Storm Clouds of Love

By Melanie Schertz

Dedicated to my dear friend, Pat Weston, for all of her work editing this story as well as her encouragement in my writing.

Also dedicated to my family, whose love has helped me through the rough times in my life.

Thank you, Jane Austen, for giving us beloved characters that have been with us for 200 years and still loved dearly.

This is a work of fiction, the story and its characters are not based upon real people or events. Any similarities are unintentional.

Chapter 1

Fitzwilliam Darcy, Master of Pemberley, England's most eligible bachelor, could not imagine how things could have gone so miserably wrong for him. It was with a sigh that he realized that within a few hours, he would be joining his cousin, Colonel Richard Fitzwilliam, would be setting off in their carriage for London, and leaving behind his disastrous visit at the home of their aunt. They had been visiting Rosing Park, the estate of Lady Catherine de Bourgh and her daughter, Anne, as the cousins had for many years.

This year, Darcy had looked forward to the visit. The previous few months had been agonizing for him, and it all began the fall the previous year. Darcy had accompanied his oldest and closest friend, Charles Bingley, to Hertfordshire to an estate which Bingley was leasing. Bingley had never had an estate to run, having his family fortune derived from trade. Bingley had asked his friend for advice, for Darcy had been the master of his estate for five years, as well as trained for his position for years previously. Bingley was in desperate need of support, as Bingley's family was of no aid to him.

Bingley was the only son, having two sisters, both of which were older than he. The eldest, Louisa, was married to a Mr. Hurst. The other sister, Caroline, was unmarried, but had her sights on capturing Mr. Darcy and Pemberley. Her pursuit of Bingley's friend at every possible chance was aggravating, as Darcy had made his point quite clear; he had absolutely no desire for an attachment with Caroline Bingley.

When Darcy, Bingley, and Bingley's sisters and brother in law all went to stay at Netherfield Hall, near Meryton, the lives of the friends would change forever. Bingley instantly fell in love with a local lady, the eldest of five daughters of a country gentleman. Miss Jane Bennet was a quiet and sweet young lady, good natured and pretty. Darcy found himself shocked at his response to meeting Jane Bennet's next eldest sister, Elizabeth. Elizabeth Bennet was as dark as her sister was fair, and where Jane was quiet and sweet, Elizabeth was fiery and quick witted. Elizabeth did not shy away from a challenge, she faced it head on. Elizabeth had been raised as the son her father did not have, educated by her father and she had a thirst for books.

Since he was not blessed with having a son and heir, Mr. Bennet's estate was entailed to his only male relative. Mr. Collins, who was a distant cousin, was a parson. While Darcy was at Netherfield, Mr. Collins had come to meet his Bennet relations. He had come to Longbourn, the Bennet estate, in hopes of finding a bride from amongst his cousins. Where he was to inherit their father's estate and become a gentleman, he felt that his cousins would not only be eager, but grateful for his attentions, which could not have been further from the truth. Mr. Collins was the type of bootlicking men who tried to kiss up to raise himself in society. It just so happened that Mr. Collins was the parson of none other than

Lady Catherine, and Mr. Collins was quite fond of speaking of her being his patroness. Jane Bennet, it was told to Mr. Collins by Mrs. Bennet, was soon to be attached, as they expected Bingley to make an offer very soon. When Mr. Collins turned his affections towards Elizabeth, he was soundly put in his place, as she had no desire to settle for a marriage of convenience, let alone a marriage to someone she found very loathsome and despicable as Mr. Collins. Mr. Collins, furious with his cousins, turned his attentions toward Elizabeth's dearest friend, Charlotte Lucas, who, at the age of thirty and no prospects for marriage, was eager to find a husband and security.

While all of this was occurring at the Bennet home, Bingley's sisters were disgusted with their brother's attraction to Jane Bennet. Caroline Bingley felt that she should put a stop to this relationship, as she had hopes to see her brother marry Georgiana Darcy, Darcy's younger sister. If Caroline could bring about this marriage, she was sure that it would help pave her way to convince Darcy to marry her. She would not allow a country nobody to get in her way, especially when she noticed Darcy's growing attraction to Elizabeth.

The night of the ball at Netherfield, Caroline decided to put her plan in motion to separate her brother from Miss Bennet. The following day, she went to Darcy, just after her brother had left for London on business for a day. Darcy had watched the Bennet's the night of the ball and decided it would be best that both Bingley and he take leave of the neighborhood. Being from the first circle of society, he could not find himself married to someone of no fortune or situation, whose family members were in the law and trade. No, he needed to escape before the fine eyes of Elizabeth Bennet completely took over his mind and made him forget who he was. And if Bingley was to attach himself to Jane, Darcy knew he would be thrown into situations time and again as the sisters were very close. No, it would be better if Bingley was away from this family all together.

So Darcy aided Caroline and Louisa in their plan to keep Bingley in London, as they insisted that Jane did not have any particularities towards him. This was done repeatedly, until Bingley was having little faith in his own ability to judge people. He had been sure Jane had feelings towards him.

Just a few weeks ago, after the holidays, it was discovered that Jane Bennet was visiting London, staying with her aunt and uncle in Cheapside. She paid a call on the Bingley townhouse, only to be slighted by Bingley's sisters. They did not return her visit, which was an even bigger insult to the young lady, but Darcy was well aware of the visit and had suggested that Jane was wasting her time.

Finally, it was time to leave London for his annual visit. What a surprise it was to learn that Elizabeth Bennet was visiting her cousin and his bride in the parsonage of Hunsford, which was attached to Rosing. He left one place to forget her only to come face to face with her.

Once he was around the lady, he decided that he wished to know more about her. He practiced to be able to converse with her, as she had suggested. Then the previous night, when she was at the parsonage alone, he came to ask for her hand in marriage. His declaration was poorly executed and even more poorly received. Elizabeth was angered. She had learned of his role in separating her sister from Bingley and decided that he had also been cruel to George Wickham and made accusations to Darcy to that matter.

George Wickham. This was a name he wished he had never heard of in his life. How one man could be such a thorn in Darcy's life, in so many ways, was surprising. So after leaving Elizabeth at the parsonage, Darcy went to his rooms and decided to write a letter to Elizabeth. At first Darcy was only going to address his beliefs that her sister felt no attachment to Bingley and that was the reason for his behavior in separating the couple. But, as he began to write, Darcy could not keep the truth from pouring out on the pages, including the truth of George Wickham.

Darcy grew up with Wickham, as the young Wickham's father was the steward for Darcy's father. Mr. Wickham died when Wickham was quite young, and as the two boys had grown up together, Mr. Darcy decided to send Wickham off to school with Darcy, treating the boy like he would his own son. This only started the never ending torture which Darcy had to endure for many years. Darcy's own father died when Darcy was a mere two and twenty. In his will, he had left Wickham a generous living of the parsonage at Kympton. When Wickham determined he did not wish to take orders, he asked for a different inheritance. He was granted the sum of three thousand pounds. Then Wickham made requests nearly twice a year for additional funds. When he was denied, Wickham became furious.

Wickham's next way of torturing Darcy was far worse. Georgiana was only ten when her father died, leaving her brother and cousin as her guardians. Just the summer before, when Georgiana was five and ten, she went to Ramsgate with her companion for a holiday. Unknown to either of the Darcy's, Wickham and the companion had made a pact to share Georgiana's dowry after they convinced the young girl to run away and elope with Wickham. Fortunately Darcy had arrived unannounced and ruined this plan. Unfortunately though, Darcy did not arrive in time to prevent Georgiana's broken heart.

In the fall, as Darcy was trying to keep from falling in love with Elizabeth, Wickham joined the militia which was being housed in Meryton. Wickham began to spread his lies about Darcy and even about Georgiana. Elizabeth had been victim of Wickham's attentions, and she had obviously fallen prey to his lies.

So, all of his dealings with Wickham began to pour out on to the paper as he wrote Elizabeth this letter. He spent so many hours as he wrote, then read the letter, making corrections, and reading again. He wished to present the letter to Elizabeth before he and Fitzwilliam left for London.

So now he was on his way back to the house to leave with his cousin. Soon they would be miles away, and Darcy would try to put his life back together after making such a disaster of it. He was not far from the house when a sudden rain storm broke loose and made vision near impossible. Fortunately he knew his way and was soon inside the house, though soaked through to the bone. The storm was ferocious and unrelenting, just as the storm inside of Darcy was. Darcy knew that Elizabeth walked in the park around the parsonage every morning, so he had waited there for her to show up on one of her favorite trails. Once she did, he stepped forward and placed the letter in her hand, asking her to please read it. Darcy then turned and walked back to Rosings.

Chapter 2

"Well, cousin, it appears we will have to wait until the storm is let up before we dare try to leave. I cannot even see the park from the windows, the rain is obscuring the view." Fitzwilliam was standing in Darcy's room waiting for him. "Good God, man, were you out of doors when the storm struck?"

"Obviously, Richard, I was and need to change my clothes. Where is Rogers?" Darcy decided to request a hot bath to take the chill away.

"I think he went down to speak to the kitchen staff about the basket we were to take with us. Would you like me to ring for him?" Darcy nodded, as Fitzwilliam was nearest the cord to pull.

A matter of moments later, Darcy's ever faithful valet returned to the master's room to find him starting to remove the wet clothing. Darcy looked at the man who had cared for his personal needs for nearly eight years and shook his head.

"Sorry, old man, but it appears that I will require some assistance. The storm has done damage to my clothing. And I think that a hot bath would help take any chill away and prevent any illness. Since we are not going anywhere until the storm abates, would you see to this?"

"Of course, sir. I will order the bath prepared immediately. Would you care to have your robe while you await the water? You really should remove the wet items and need something to put on."

"If you haven't already packed it, I would appreciate it."

The valet left the room to make the preparations and to retrieve the robe as well as fresh clothes for after the bath.

"So William, what were you doing outside? We were to leave shortly, and I had wished to go down to say our farewells to the parsonage before we left. I thought you would wish to go with me."

"I desired a walk to burn off some energy before entering the carriage. I had not thought about going to the parsonage. If you wish, when the storm relents, and we prepare to leave, we might stop there as we pass out of the park."

Fitzwilliam was watching his cousin pacing and staring out the window at the rain. He had a curiosity as to what was on his mind, as he had noticed a change come over Darcy in the presence of Elizabeth Bennet. "I shall be sad to leave here this year. I have never enjoyed myself here at Rosing like I have this year. Amazing how much different a lovely young lady can make on the visit."

Darcy turned and glared at his cousin. "So you have enjoyed a certain young lady's company have you?"

"How could any man not enjoy such a delightful person?"

Darcy growled at his cousin's remark and went back to staring out into the rain. It had not slowed at all, and visibility was nil.

While Darcy soaked in the hot tub of water, Fitzwilliam went downstairs to check with their carriage driver. The driver stated that there would be no way to leave that day because of the storm, even if it was to cease soon. The roads would be extremely muddy and would be dangerous to travel. Fitzwilliam relayed the information to his aunt and was preparing to return upstairs to tell Darcy when a message arrived from the parsonage. A servant was sent to inquire if Elizabeth had taken refuge from the storm at Rosing, for no one knew where she was and she had not been seen since she set off for a walk quite early, long before the storm struck.

Fitzwilliam ran up the stairs to inquire if Darcy had seen Elizabeth when he had been in the park earlier. When he walked into his cousin's dressing room, Darcy had a concerned look for his cousin. "What has happened Fitzwilliam? Are Aunt Catherine and Anne well?"

Fitzwilliam took a breath. "It is not Aunt Catherine or Anne. We just received word from the parsonage inquiring if Miss Elizabeth was here, as no one has seen her since before she set out for a walk in the park this morning."

Color drained from Darcy's face, as he raced to his bedchamber's windows. His heart stopped as he saw the rain was still as violent as it had been when he entered the house. Elizabeth was in this storm. How was she ever to find her way back to the parsonage in this rain? Had she continued to walk after he left her, and in which direction had she gone? So many questions ran through his mind.

"I saw her in the park, and she was quite a distance from the parsonage at that time. I am not sure in which direction she was planning going. She was near the section where the path leads to the large hill and the river. We must begin to search for her immediately."

"William, the only reason the servant was able to arrive here from the parsonage was because of the storm rope. There is no visibility out there. We could walk two feet from Miss Elizabeth and not know she was there unless we stumbled over her. I will send the servant back with word that we will begin the search as soon as the storm lets up. She will be fine; she is probably hidden in one of the caves near the hill. Probably a little wet, but otherwise, she is fine."

"I was out there when it began. Had I not known where I was and been so familiar, I would have lost my way. This storm is relentless. In it, you can see nothing because it blinds you. She was not dressed to be in such rain, and would probably not have been able to make her way to the caves unless it was by some miracle."

"Hold faith, William. There is nothing we can do until the storm lets up." Fitzwilliam was amazed at his cousin's behavior. "I am surprised at the level of your concern for Miss Elizabeth. Would you care to enlighten me of where it comes?"

"I have no idea what you are speaking of, Richard." Darcy stated to his cousin without looking at him. When there was no response from Fitzwilliam, Darcy finally turned and looked at his cousin. A raised brow told Darcy that though others might accept this, Fitzwilliam would not. "If you insist on knowing, we best get something to drink and have a seat, for it is a long story."

It was nearly two hours later when Darcy finished telling Fitzwilliam of his feelings, his time in Hertfordshire, the disastrous marriage proposal, and the letter. The rain had still continued beating at the window, reminding Darcy with every moment that Elizabeth was out of doors and trapped by the storm, as another storm raged inside his heart.

"Do you know if she read your letter?" Fitzwilliam asked. "I am more than happy to confirm any of the details of which I am aware, especially in concerns to Georgiana and Wickham. You must be in love if you opened your heart to her and wrote of his betrayal."

Darcy nodded. "Not even Bingley knows of all that I wrote to Miss Elizabeth."

"I must ask for your forgiveness, cousin. I realize now that I may have been the reason she became so furious last night."

Darcy frowned and looked at his cousin. "How so? You were not there when I made such a fool of myself in my proposal."

"But I had spoken with her earlier in the day. I spoke of how devoted you were to those who you hold dear. And I held your story of coming to Bingley's aid as evidence of your devotion. I had no idea of the young lady being Miss Elizabeth's sister, as you gave me no name of the young lady. I am so truly sorry for saying anything; I thought I was showing what a devoted friend and family member you are."

"It is not your fault Richard. I did an unspeakable wrong to Miss Bennet and Bingley, and through them, I have injured Miss Elizabeth. I alone am responsible for my behavior. I just fear that Miss Elizabeth is paying for my behavior now, as she might have been closer to safety had I not stopped her in the park to give her the letter. What if she stopped to read the letter? I am guilty of keeping her out of doors which has now placed her health in jeopardy."

"William, you cannot take the weight of all the wrongs in the world onto your shoulders. It is not possible for you to be responsible for everything which happens. We must hold onto faith that she will be fine."

Looking out at the storm Darcy shook his head. "How could you or I be fine in such weather, let alone a young lady such as Miss Elizabeth? No, I fear I have done Miss Elizabeth a grave misfortune by ever having met her."

Rogers brought a tray of food to the men later in the day, and kept them updated as to the preparations which were being made in the house to search for Elizabeth as soon as possible. As evening came, and the storm showed no sign of relenting, Darcy's mood became darker than ever. He had no desire to be around his aunt, for he did not wish to hear her opinion of Elizabeth being out of doors when the storm struck. He also did not wish to be comforted, as he knew that Elizabeth was not being comforted at this moment, so why should he?

Fitzwilliam decided to stay with Darcy that night as they sat up in Darcy's sitting room. Both dozed off and on, but neither used their bedchambers, as they napped in the chairs of the sitting room. They could hear the storm still raging outside the window, and Fitzwilliam was concerned as each hour went by if they would find Elizabeth alive. He tried to be positive to his cousin, but having lived the life of a soldier for many years, he also knew the reality of life. Elizabeth was a strong and healthy young lady. But this storm was more than a strong and healthy young lady, dressed for a walk on a pleasant spring morning, could bear up under, let alone if she had become injured. What would Darcy do if Elizabeth was to die?

Fitzwilliam had never seen his cousin in such a state, even after the dealings with Wickham after Ramsgate. Elizabeth had become so dear to Darcy, for Darcy to wish to marry her was shocking. Now, when the woman Darcy desired to spend his life with was so near, yet he could not reach her to protect her, it was painful to watch the Master of Pemberley in such agony.

Chapter 3

It was near two in the afternoon the following day did the storm let up to allow the search to begin. There was great fear as to what they would find, after Elizabeth had been missing for more than a full day. The search began at the location where Darcy had last seen Elizabeth, then worked in different directions from there. Many of the servants from Rosing had come to aid in the search. It took an hour for them to locate Elizabeth, and the sight nearly killed Darcy.

In her disoriented state, Elizabeth had ended up on the path of the hill. The hill was tall, and there was no way to reach the bottom without climbing down with ropes. The river ran near the base, and with the rains, had swelled over the banks. Elizabeth had fallen from the top of the hill, and now lay at the bottom, near the river. There was no movement, and blood was visible on her face. Darcy was frantic, as only his cousin holding onto him kept him from climbing down the face of the hill without any ropes.

Fitzwilliam called to the searchers, sending them to Rosing to bring a stretcher, ropes and a wagon to the park. He also sent another servant to the parsonage and requested the surgeon be sent to Rosings to be prepared for when they brought Elizabeth there. He kept a hold of his cousin, refusing to let go of Darcy for even a moment. "I know she is alive, William. Hold on to your hopes. Do not lose faith that she is alive."

"Richard, look at her. She does not move. She is bleeding and broken. How could she possibly be alive? How? I am to blame. It is my fault that she did not reach safety before the storm struck. I will never forgive myself for this."

"Get a hold of yourself, William. You need to be strong for her. When we get down to her, and when we bring her back to Rosings, she will need you and your strength. William, I know you can be that strong. It will not be long before the servants are returned with the ropes and stretcher and you and I will go down to Miss Elizabeth."

Darcy nodded his head. "Thank you Richard. How do you wish to go down? Should we tie the ropes to the trees?"

"No, I was thinking that we should bring the wagon back to here, and then tie the ropes to it. So when we are ready to come up, the wagon can be used to aid in pulling us up."

"Will the wagon make it this far? Or would it be better to tie to the harness of the horses?"

"I remember a wagon being here before, but if we are unable to bring it so far as we need, then we will use the horses."

As they spoke, the wagon arrived with all that was necessary for the men to make their way down the hillside, with Fitzwilliam making the trip first. Once at the bottom, Fitzwilliam checked to ensure Elizabeth was alive. To his great relief, Elizabeth was indeed alive. Darcy quickly arrived beside his cousin, and kneeled down to Elizabeth. He gently picked her up, and waited for the stretcher to be placed for him to lay her on it. He could tell from the angle of her leg that it was broken, and there was a nasty gash on the side of her head which was bleeding. Darcy tore off his cravat and applied it to the wound. Once she was placed on the stretcher and tied tightly to it, the men had the wagon pull the ropes forward to bring the threesome up the hill.

They quickly placed Elizabeth on the back of the wagon, and then covered her with several blankets. Darcy jumped on the back of the wagon as Fitzwilliam sat on the bench with the driver. The trip back was taken slowly because of the conditions of the land and the wish to not injure Elizabeth any further. Upon their arrival at the house, Elizabeth was taken directly into the infirmary. The doctor had arrived and was awaiting the arrival of his patient. Darcy and Fitzwilliam carried the stretcher into the infirmary, and Darcy instantly grabbed a bowl of water and some cloths and began to wash the blood and dirt from Elizabeth's face. Doctor Lyndon began to inspect her injuries. The cut on her head would require stitching, and he would have to set her leg. All of the other injuries appeared to be minor in comparison, small cuts, abrasions, bruising. The next few days would be quite painful for her as she began to feel all of the injuries.

"Mr. Darcy, if you would request one of the men servants to come assist me, I need to set her leg before we do anything else. Then I will need the ladies to assist in taking her into the bathing chamber to clean her. I will come to you when I know more information."

"No, I will stay here and be of assistance. What do you need me to do while you set her leg?"

"It is not appropriate sir, and your aunt will not be pleased if you were to stay. The servants will be able to aid me with Miss Elizabeth's care."

"I have told you that I will be staying. Now stop wasting time and let us get Miss Elizabeth's leg set." Shaking his head, Doctor Lyndon realized he would have to deal with the disapproval of Lady Catherine at a later time, for he was not ready to deal with disagreeing with Mr. Darcy right then.

"Mr. Darcy, if you would lift her and sit behind her so that you can hold onto her and prevent her from lurching as I maneuver her bone back into place. It will be quite painful and we need to keep her as still as possible."

Darcy moved behind Elizabeth, bringing her to a seated position with his arms around her, holding her to him tightly.

"I am ready, Doctor."

As Doctor Lyndon moved the bone into place, Elizabeth woke with a scream. "Miss Elizabeth, please hold still. You are safe and at Rosings in the infirmary. The doctor is setting your broken leg bone. Just remain calm and let us take care of you."

"Mr. Darcy, is that you?" Darcy nodded and leaned his mouth closer to her ear.

"Have no fear of my being here, I just wished to be of assistance to you."

"I could never fear you Mr. Darcy. I am actually quite pleased to have you with me. It brings me comfort."

Darcy could not prevent the smile he felt at her words. "I will be at your side as long as you wish, Miss Elizabeth."

"Mr. Darcy, I wish for you to remain with me. I am so truly sorrowed as to how I treated you. I read the letter."

The doctor gave his patient a puzzled look, as he continued to splint her leg.

"Miss Elizabeth, as much as I am pleased to hear this, it also grieves me that it kept you out of doors which led to your injuries. Please forgive me."

"As you have no control over the weather, how can you be held responsible? I saw no signs before the storm struck. One moment was bright and nice, the next the heavens opened and poured down. So there is nothing to forgive. That is, unless you have changed your mind from the other night."

Darcy held his breath. Could he possibly be hearing what he thought he was? Could Elizabeth be speaking of his disaster of a proposal? "Of what are you speaking which I would possibly have changed my mind? Are you referring to my ridiculous stumbling over my tongue the other night at the parsonage?"

"I am indeed. Have you changed your mind?"

"I have not changed my mind as to what I asked you. Could I be so blessed as to your opinion being different? Have you, perhaps, changed your mind?"

With her head leaning back against Darcy's shoulder, she winced in pain as the doctor continued working on her leg. "I have indeed. I have had much to think of this past day. I realized how horribly wrong I was. May I have a second chance at answering your question?"

Darcy held his breath. "Miss Elizabeth Bennet, may I have the great honor of asking for you to give me the greatest joy and agree to be my wife?"

A weak smile graced her face as she looked at Doctor Lyndon. Taking Darcy's hand in hers, Elizabeth nodded slightly. "My answer is yes. Yes, I will marry you."

Darcy squeezed her hand slightly. "I am now the happiest man in the world. Thank you my dearest. I do love you."

"And I have learned just how dearly I love you. It is amazing what it took for me to realize the truth."

Doctor Lyndon looked at the couple. "Now, Mr. Darcy, if you would be so kind as to carry your betrothed into the bathing chamber, I will have the servants clean Miss Elizabeth properly and we will finish repairing her injuries. But I will ask that you step into the hallway as she is being cleaned and dressed. I will not have your aunt sending for the tar and feathers to dunk me in from her displeasure."

Darcy realized he had completely disregarded the rules of propriety and had technically compromised Elizabeth. "As you wish Doctor." Leaning Elizabeth onto the table in the bathing chamber, he placed a light kiss on her forehead. "It is a good thing you accepted me, for the doctor would have had to have me flogged for my behavior." He smiled at the small spark in her eyes. Even as much pain as she suffered, she was still able to dazzle him. "I will be back in a little while. You have brought me the greatest joy today. Of course that was after making my heart stop beating when I first saw you at the base of the hill."

"I never stated that I would be an easy person to be in love with, did I?"

With a smile, Darcy removed from the room. As soon as he was in the hallway, he was informed that he was required in the drawing room immediately. Darcy knew what was coming, as his aunt would be highly displeased with his behavior. First, he was one of the people to go down the hill to retrieve Elizabeth, then, riding with her to Rosings, but to top it all off, being in the infirmary with Elizabeth and the doctor while she was being cared for. He steeled himself for the ranting he knew his aunt would begin the moment she saw him.

Fitzwilliam was waiting outside the drawing room for Darcy. "How is Miss Elizabeth? Will she recover?"

"Elizabeth will recover. She has a broken leg, a head wound and many other minor cuts and bumps. She will be in a great deal of pain for a while, but will recover."

"Cousin, I know that I have not said anything up until now about your improper behavior, but to refer to Miss Elizabeth improperly will be highly unacceptable behavior."

"But, it is not improper behavior for me to refer to my fiancé in such a manner." Darcy's smile made his dimples stand out beautifully.

"Did you say fiancé? Are you telling me that she has accepted you?"

"As the doctor as my witness, yes. Elizabeth has indeed accepted my request for her hand. She read my letter and had some, well, time on her hands to do nothing but think. She decided that she truly had feelings for me, but had not allowed them to surface for her anger with me over her sister."

"And how do you wish to approach our aunt?"

"I will tell her the truth. She can either accept it, or she can disown me as family. It is her decision."

Darcy walked into the drawing room to hear his aunt begin her tirade. "William, what is the meaning of this behavior I have been told of? Have you been forward in your behavior in regards to Miss Elizabeth Bennet?"

"I have been involved in the search for her, and once found, Richard and I were the ones to climb down to retrieve her. We brought her here for care and I have just come from the infirmary from assisting Doctor Lyndon in setting Elizabeth's broken leg bone. I am now waiting for the ladies to bath her, dress her and return her to the bed. Then I will return to the infirmary to be by her side."

"William, this is highly improper. You need to stop this immediately. We cannot have any gossip injure you and my daughter before you can even marry."

"Aunt Catherine, I have told you time and again, I will not marry Anne. Anne has also told you, as well as Uncle Henry and Aunt Elaine, and even Richard here has told you. I have proposed to and been accepted by Elizabeth Bennet and will be marrying her as soon as possible. I do not wish to hear anymore about my duty to marry Anne and the plan of you and my mother to unite the two estates. It was only your dream, never anyone else's."

"How dare you speak to me so? I am your nearest relative, and you owe me your respect. Have you learned such behavior from Miss Bennet? I wish for her to be removed from my home immediately. She is to be moved to the doctor's office this very moment. She will not be welcome in my home ever again.

Nor will she be welcome in the parsonage, as I will demand Mr. Collins to disown his relations immediately."

"As you well know, you have no right to force Mr. Collins from disowning his family, especially his inheritance. I will not endanger my fiancé's health by moving her. You will have to accept this or refuse to speak with me ever again. It matters not to me. But Elizabeth will remain in the infirmary until she has recovered to a point she can safely be moved."

"It will not be had. This is my home and I refuse to accept this. If you will not remove her then I will have my servants do so. Send her on her way to her family and their home."

"NO!" The voice came from beside Lady Catherine. "Mother, how dare you try and run William's life. You have indeed been told that I will not marry William, as I have no desire to do so. I am thrilled for William and Miss Elizabeth. And as this has been my home for the past two years, I have the right to decide who is and who is not welcome here. If you persist, I will take steps to have you moved to the dowager house."

"See what this upstart has brought upon you William? Now you have even forced Anne into your unheard of behavior. I will not stand for this. I am sending for your uncle to come talk sense into you. In the mean time, I do insist you remove that vile ingrate from my home this moment."

"Now I have to step up and stand beside my cousins here." Fitzwilliam stood and walked over to Darcy and Anne, the three cousins standing side by side. "I have already sent a messenger to my father regarding the situation of Miss Elizabeth's accident and requesting they come quickly as William here would need their support."

"I am not speaking to you two, I am speaking with William. Anne, take Richard and leave the room so I may finish my discussion with William."

"No, mother. We will remain. If anyone is to leave, it will be you. I have decided to take up the inheritance I was left by father and have until now allowed you to control. No longer though, as I am now the lady of the estate. If I were you mother, I would be preparing my belongings for the move. I will have the dowager house opened and ready for you within a week."

Looking at Darcy, Lady Catherine was furious. "How dare you come to my home and abuse my hospitality? You bring this country nobody here and take away my own daughter's chance for happiness. You turn your cousins against me, making my own daughter desire to remove me from my home. How dare you call yourself my family? I will never acknowledge you again."

"Aunt Catherine, you have been told by Anne, William and myself of the truth. It is you who refuses to accept the truth. William and Elizabeth are to marry. Anne is taking her rightful position as Lady Anne of Rosings. You will be moved in one week to the dowager house. I have sent for my parents to come, and I know that they will be pleased for William when they hear the news and meet his choice in brides."

"Mother, it is time for you to go to your suite and begin your preparations. When Uncle Henry and Aunt Elaine arrive, I will have them come to your rooms. I will also have Uncle Henry contact the family attorney to prepare the paperwork for your move to your new accommodations as well as for me to take my inheritance fully."

Full of anger for the country upstart she held responsible for the three young members of her family to have so turned against her, Lady Catherine stormed from the drawing room to her apartment to await her brother's arrival. She had faith that Lord Matlock would put the situation to rights.

After Lady Catherine left the room, Darcy turned to his cousins with great appreciation. "Anne, how can I ever thank you for your support? And you, Richard, did you really write to your parents and ask them to come? You are both truly the dearest relations I could ever ask for."

"William, you are like a brother to me, more so than Matthew has ever been. You told me your relationship with Elizabeth, all that you struggled with. And then sitting with you all of last night and holding you from clawing your way down the hillside to get to her, I knew that you truly loved your lady. You are a good man, cousin. Elizabeth will be quite lucky to have you for a husband. Of course I would write to my parents to come, even before we left to search for Elizabeth. I knew what Aunt Catherine's reaction would be to all of this."

"And it is about time that I stood up to my mother. She has long ignored the wishes of others and it is time she learned the consequences for her behavior. William, I am so pleased that you have found someone to love. Miss Elizabeth is remarkable."

"My thanks to both of you. I need to return to the infirmary. I do not wish to be away from Elizabeth for long."

After nodding to his cousins, Darcy quickly left the room. He knew he needed to send word to Longbourn to Elizabeth's father, as well as to Georgiana and to Bingley. He had so much to atone for with Bingley. If all went well, he would put his friend back on the road to his own future with his own Bennet sister.

When Darcy arrived outside the infirmary door, Doctor Lyndon was just coming out. "Mr. Darcy, I was just coming to see you. Your betrothed has fallen asleep. I am concerned, though, of her developing a fever. The weather may have had a diabolical affect on Miss Elizabeth, but we will have to wait and watch closely. With her weakness at this moment, a high fever could prove to be fatal."

This was like a knife driven into Darcy's chest. "What can we do to prevent this?"

"All we can do is keep her comfortable, encourage her to take nourishment, and keep a close eye on her wounds for signs of infection. I will send for another bottle of laudanum, for she will be in a great deal of pain for some time. Now, as I have said for her, you also need to take nourishment. You will be of no aid to Miss Elizabeth if you do not take care of yourself as well. While she is asleep, you should rest as well. I will send someone to find you when she wakes."

"I will remain here; I have no desire to be away from her, especially up in my rooms."

Anne had just walked up to hear the last statements made. "Cousin, this suite of rooms, across the hall, were once guest rooms. We now use them for storage. I will have them cleaned out and furniture brought in for your personal use. You will be able to rest there, and as needed, you will have the use of the sitting room of the suite."

Darcy looked at his cousin. "Anne, I cannot begin to thank you for everything you have done for Elizabeth and myself. I have never given you the proper credit you deserve."

"My dear cousin, you just did. I cannot imagine not doing everything possible for you and your dear Elizabeth. She is an amazing young lady and I am quite happy for you to have found her."

Chapter 4

Anne then turned to a passing servant and requested her housekeeper sent immediately. "Doctor, did you require someone sent to retrieve items from your office? I will have a servant sent for you. If there is anything you will require, all you need to do is ask, as my staff will be at your disposal."

When the housekeeper arrived in the hall, Anne made a list of what she insisted to be done, a runner for the doctor, the suite of rooms cleared of the storage, which Anne requested moved to the ballroom, and furniture brought to make the suite comfortable for Darcy. Rogers prepared to have Darcy's personal items moved.

Darcy stepped back into the infirmary while all the work was being done. He brought with him paper and pen, to write the letters he knew he should. Looking at Elizabeth lying so still, looking so pale, Darcy was deeply concerned. The doctor's words continued to run through his head. If Elizabeth was to develop a high fever while she was so very weak, she could die from it. Fatal, the doctor's word continued to play over and over in Darcy's mind. To loose her now, after all of the time Darcy had wasted in denying his love for her, would crush Darcy. He had no desire to live a life that did not include Elizabeth at his side. Darcy reached out a hand, caressing the right side of her face gently. Her skin was as soft as he had always imagined. Even with all the injuries, she was still so beautiful. Darcy took a hold of her hand, lifting it to his lips and placing a loving kiss on the palm. "Stay with me Elizabeth. Do not leave me now that we have found each other."

Without opening her eyes, a smile graced her lips. "I do not wish to leave you, Mr. Darcy."

"William, dearest. Not Mr. Darcy anymore."

"My William. I do not desire to leave you."

"Doctor Lyndon says you need to eat and rest. Let me send for some broth. After that I insist on your sleeping. I will be at your side while you rest."

"And you will also need to eat and rest, my William. Please do take care of yourself. I do not wish for you to take ill because of me."

Darcy laughed. "As you command, my love. You have control of my heart so I must do whatever you say."

Elizabeth was still smiling, though she had not opened her eyes as they spoke. "Rest, my love. Let me send for the broth for you." He stepped to the door and sent word for the kitchen staff for the broth and some tea.

Surprisingly the staff had already prepared the broth and the tray arrived within moments of Darcy requesting it. He laughed as he saw that the tray was for two, obviously others were determined that he take some broth and tea as well. Elizabeth was able to take some of the broth, though not very much. She still had not opened her eyes and

Darcy could tell it took all of her strength to make even the most simple of efforts.

Once she had finished the broth she could take, Darcy lay her head back on the pillow and placed a kiss of her forehead. "Sleep my love. I will be here when you wake."

"But you need to sleep as well, William. You should go to your rooms and sleep. I will be fine. Someone will come to you when I am awake again."

"No, I am not leaving you. As we speak, Anne is having the suite across the hall cleared of storage and prepared for me to use. So I will not be far from you until you are well enough to throw me out yourself." He smiled at his fiancé.

"Well then, I know you will always be near me since I could never lift you enough to be able to throw you." There was a smile gracing her impertinent lips.

"I guess there are benefits to keeping you somewhat weakened then."

Elizabeth drifted off to sleep with her fiancé holding tightly to her hand. Instead of writing the letters he knew he should, Darcy dozed off in the chair beside her bed. It was a fitful rest, as visions of Elizabeth lying at the bottom of the hill continued to run through his mind. Only in his visions, he saw her broken body and found her to be lifeless.

When Darcy woke, he found Doctor Lyndon checking on Elizabeth's condition.

"Mr. Darcy, I am afraid that Miss Elizabeth has developed a slight fever. We must work to keep it from becoming any worse."

"What do we need to do?" The concern was written on Darcy's face.

"We need to begin with placing cloths which have been dipped in cold water on her forehead. We will need the coldest water we can get. If it continues to grow, we will need to send for some ice."

"I will find the servants and request what we need. I also need to speak with my cousin and have him send some expresses."

Darcy stepped out into the hallway, the fear written on his face. A servant passing by quickly went to find Fitzwilliam, and sent another for the cloths and bowls of cold water.

Fitzwilliam came quickly to his cousin when he heard Darcy was in need of him immediately. As it was rare for Darcy to ask for aid, Fitzwilliam knew that the situation was dire.

"Richard, I need to have you send express riders to Longbourn and to Georgiana. Mr. Bennet needs to be made aware of his daughter's injuries and that she has begun to develop a fever which will be very dangerous for her. I wish Georgiana to come with your parents if they have not already left. I guess you should send word to your parents as well."

"I will do this immediately. What else can I do?"

"Pray cousin. As weak as Elizabeth is, if the fever takes a strong hold on her, the doctor fears she will not survive."

"Hold on to hope, William. She will be well again soon. I have faith that Elizabeth will survive."

As Darcy turned to enter the infirmary he had another thought. "Richard, send another express for me as well. It is to Bingley. Just tell him that I have requested he come immediately, do not tell him anything about Elizabeth. He is in London right now at his townhouse."

Fitzwilliam knew what his cousin wished to discuss with Bingley. "I will get the letters done immediately. Trust that Elizabeth will recover."

Nodding his head, Darcy returned to Elizabeth's side. Fitzwilliam wrote the letters quickly, informing Mr. Bennet of his daughter's injuries and developing fever. This letter he sent off before beginning the others. He quickly wrote to Georgiana that William had some news for his sister and because he knew that Fitzwilliam had written to his parents to come to Rosing, asked Fitzwilliam to invite Georgiana to come with them. Then Fitzwilliam wrote the letter to Bingley. He decided to make the letter very urgent, to bring Bingley to Rosing immediately.

It was near midnight when the express rider pounded on the door of Longbourn. Mr. Bennet received the letter, then hurried up the stairs to inform his wife and daughters of Elizabeth's plight. A letter was quickly written to inform of Mr. Bennet and his daughters Jane and Mary arrival which was expected to be by five the next afternoon. Quickly, Mr. Bennet and his daughters packed as their carriage was prepared. The younger two daughters and Mrs. Bennet would remain at Longbourn. Mr. Bennet was pleased that they did not wish to travel, as he knew Elizabeth would recover faster without her mother and youngest silliness and shrill voices.

Mrs. Hill, who had been the family's devoted housekeeper for many years, had tears in her eyes as she watched her master and his daughters leave. She then turned back to care for Mrs. Bennet who insisted on attentions for her palpitations from worry. Mrs. Bennet could not allow her daughter's dire health concerns to take all the attention.

Georgiana received her express at the same time as her aunt and uncle, who were with her as they had just returned to the Fitzwilliam townhouse after an evening at the theatre. Georgiana's was somewhat light, not informing her of her brother's engagement or his fiancé's condition. In his letter to his parents, Fitzwilliam told of Elizabeth's injuries and that she had developed a fever. He told them of the doctor's concern due to Elizabeth's weakness. He also told them of her acceptance of Darcy's hand and the subsequent argument with Lady Catherine. The news was shocking to the Fitzwilliam's, and they decided that they must leave at first light to make their way. They would wait until the long ride to bring Georgiana up to date on the events.

Bingley had just prepared to retire for the evening when the knock on his door alerted his attention. He took the express and after quickly reading the message, told the express rider to take the message back that he was on his way. A carriage would be too slow, as Bingley felt the urgency in the letter from Colonel Fitzwilliam. For Darcy to request his cousin to write the letter pleading with Bingley to come to Rosings immediately could only mean Darcy was in the gravest of situations. He must have met with a terrible accident or taken horribly ill for such a letter to have been sent.

Bingley ordered his horse prepared immediately as he ran up the stairs to pack some items into saddle bags. He left a note for his sisters for when they woke that he had to leave on urgent business and would be away for an unknown length of time. He had no desire to tell them that Darcy was in dire straights, for Caroline would be on the next carriage to follow after. Bingley did not wish for his sister to cause his friend any further distress by having Caroline fawning over him.

Bingley rode nonstop to Rosing, as he feared his friend being on death's doorstep. Upon his arriving at the house, he was quickly shown into the sitting room across from the infirmary. Fitzwilliam was seated there, waiting for any of the guests who where on their way.

"Bingley, how good to see you. You look as if you rode here on horseback."

"I did. I admit that when I received your express, I could not imagine why I was needed, and then I came to the realization that it was a matter of life or death for my dear friend. I could waste no time to get here to be of whatever comfort and aid I could. Now, can you tell me what has happened?"

Fitzwilliam decided that he would allow Darcy to do all the talking with Bingley. "I will be right back. Can I offer you something to drink to wash down the road so to speak?"

"Many thanks. I feel like I have swallowed enough dirt to plant a garden."

Fitzwilliam stepped across the hall to inform Darcy of Bingley's arrival. Slowly Darcy rose, placing more cold wet cloths on Elizabeth's forehead as her fever had continued to rise.

Darcy stepped through the door of the sitting room to find a very startled Bingley looking at him. "Bingley, you look a fright."

"And you appear better than I expected. I thought for sure that your cousin's express meant you were dying. So what has happened that you need me here, and you could not write the express yourself?"

"It is a long story, and one I have to beg your forgiveness and indulgence. Ah, I see my cousin has brought us a bottle." Fitzwilliam stepped into the room momentarily to place the tray containing glasses and a bottle of port on the table. "I will leave you gentlemen be. William, if you need anything, please let me know."

Chapter 5

As Darcy poured drinks for himself and Bingley, he began. "First I need to beg your forgiveness. I have done something which I know will come as a surprise and will be painful for you. When your sisters and I followed you to London last November, we lied to you. Your sisters came to me and wished to end your relationship with Miss Bennet. They felt that you were on the way to an attachment, and that you would be ridiculed by society for such a low connection. Though I was concerned about the connection, as well, I had different reasons for keeping you from an attachment with Jane Bennet."

Bingley looked at his friend confused as he listened. "While you were falling in love with one Bennet daughter, I was finding myself more and more interested with another one. I was falling in love with Elizabeth Bennet. Only my pride was keeping me from acting on my feelings, as I could not imagine marrying so far beneath my station. If you were to marry Jane Bennet, I would be constantly thrown into the path of Elizabeth, and I was afraid to admit my feelings for her. It was better to separate the two of you. I told you at the time that I did not see any feelings of being more than friendly, and I honestly did not see any partiality on her part. I have learned since, though that she was extremely partial towards you, and was devastated when you left."

"And how did you come to know this?" Bingley asked as he watched his friend.

"From Elizabeth. She has been here visiting Mr. and Mrs. Collins. Mrs. Collins is formerly Charlotte Lucas. I had no idea of Elizabeth's being at the parsonage when Richard and I came for our yearly visit. Elizabeth was furious with me for separating you from Jane and she thrashed me soundly for it. I must, also, inform you I was aware of Jane Bennet being in London for several weeks, just after the holidays. She paid a visit to your sisters, which they decided not to return. Instead they came to me for advice. At the time I did not know what would come of life now."

"And what has come now that has changed your opinion of the Bennet family?"

"Because I have finally allowed my feelings for Elizabeth to be known. I have asked Elizabeth to marry me, and after her thrashing me and some incorrect information she had about me being corrected, Elizabeth only yesterday accepted my request for her hand. We are engaged."

"I am shocked at all of this, and appalled at what you and my sisters have done. But why did you have your cousin send me the express? Obviously you could have written to me or sent to me yourself."

"I have been too busy with a situation which has prevented me from doing so. Please, follow me. You need to see this for yourself." Darcy led the way across the hall to the infirmary. At first, Bingley did not recognize the person in the bed. Finally realizing the frail and broken person as Elizabeth, and watching as Darcy took the cloth from her forehead and rinsed it in cold water before placing it back on her head, Bingley knew the urgency of his friend needing him to come to Rosing.

"What has happened to her?" Bingley asked. Darcy shook his head, and pointed towards the door. "Let us go back across the hall. She needs her rest."

When they arrived back in the sitting room, Bingley witnessed something he had never seen in his many years as Darcy's friend. He saw tears running down Darcy's face.

"As I told you, I proposed to Elizabeth. She initially turned me down. The situation with you and Jane was one of the reasons. I stayed up all night that night, writing a letter to Elizabeth, explaining my reasons for separating you, and correcting some information which had been falsely told to her. I went into the park in the early hours of the morning and waited for her to come on her daily walk. When she arrived, I gave her the letter and asked her to please read it. I then walked back towards Rosing. Just as I was near the house, a violent and unrelenting rainstorm down poured."

Taking a sip from his glass, Darcy continued. "Fortunately I knew where I was and did not need to worry about being able to see, as the rain was blinding. Unfortunately, we discovered later that Elizabeth had not made her way back to the parsonage before the storm struck. We were not able to search for her until the following afternoon, for the storm did not relent until then. When we finally found her, she had lost her way and fallen from the hill top. Richard and I had to climb down on ropes and bring her up on a stretcher. She broke her leg and had many cuts, scrapes and bruises, particularly a nasty cut on the side of her head which required stitching. We brought her here for medical care, and when she woke, she told me she had read the letter and had spent a lot of time thinking. She accepted my proposal. I am so very thrilled that she has agreed."

Darcy poured another glass of port for himself, and then walked to the doorway, looking across the hall at the closed door to where his beloved lay burning up with fever. "The worst has now happened, as she had been exposed to the rain for more than a day, laying there broken and battered, and has now developed a fever. It is taking a strong hold of her weakened body and shows no signs of letting her go. The doctor is fearful of Elizabeth being able to fight it, he has even told us that the fever could be fatal for her."

Bingley was beside himself. "But Miss Elizabeth is a strong young lady. Surely she will be able to rally herself to improve."

"If it was just the fever or just the injuries, I have no doubt. But she was so severely injured and the storm was so violent. The fever has taken a deep hold on her. The combination is too much for one person to be able to recover from. I finally win the hand of the woman I love and now I may very well loose her before we can begin our life together. So I am here to tell you. If you are in love with Jane Bennet, tell her. Do not allow anyone to tell you that your feelings are wrong; do not care of her connections. Do not loose your chance at love. I know that Jane Bennet is in love with you. If your feelings are the same, then seize the moment and marry her. Have a wonderful life together. Do not be as foolish as I have been. I am paying a very high price for my pride right now. And I never plan to allow my pride to get in the way again."

Bingley was amazed at all the information he had just learned. But what amazed him the most was the emotions that his friend was showing. Never had he seen Darcy so overwhelmed with sentiment.

"I take it that Miss Elizabeth's family has been notified of the accident."

"Richard sent word to them, and Mr. Bennet wrote back that he, Jane and Mary would be arriving here near five this afternoon. They have no knowledge of Elizabeth's fever worsening throughout the night and this day. I know that they will be devastated when they arrive and see her."

"It was difficult, at first, to realize who it was on the bed. What can be done for her?"

"Keep applying cold cloths for now. There is little else at the moment we can do. Except pray that is."

"My prayers are with both of you. I have faith, Miss Elizabeth will pull through. I know she will."

Just then, a servant came to announce the arrival of Mr. Bennet and his two daughters.

Chapter 6

Darcy met the Bennets in the hallway in front of the infirmary. He shook the hand of Mr. Bennet and led him into the sitting room. Bingley watched Jane as she had mixed emotions. She was concerned for her sister's welfare but she was also pleased to see Bingley.

"Mr. Bennet, I am deeply grieved of the need for you to travel here. Let me inform you as to what has happened. Miss Elizabeth was outside in the park for an early morning walk when a sudden and severe storm struck. I was outside near this house and only due to my being very accustomed to the area was I able to find the house as the severity of the rain made vision near impossible. Miss Elizabeth was not so fortunate. She lost her way and fell off a hill. We were made aware of her being missing, but, as the rains continued we were unable to begin the search for her until visibility was restored which was not until the following afternoon. As soon as she was located, my cousin and I brought Miss Elizabeth here to Rosings. We had sent for the surgeon to meet us here and I knew that the infirmary here was well stocked. Miss Elizabeth has a nasty gash on the side of her head, a broken left leg, and many other cuts and bumps. She was extremely sore when she came to, which was as the doctor set the broken bones in her leg. Since then, she has developed a severe fever. The doctor and I have worked constantly to control the fever, but to no success."

"And why sir would you personally be involved in my daughter's care?" Mr. Bennet raised his eyebrow and searched for answers in Darcy's expression.

Looking straight into Mr. Bennet's eyes, Darcy took a deep breath. "Because sir, I am in love with your daughter. I had proposed to her the previous night and was refused, for reasons I will not elaborate on at this moment, though I would be willing speak in private with you later about it. I wrote her a letter concerning her issues against marrying me and had presented it to her as she was walking in the park the morning of the storm. I later discovered from Miss Elizabeth that she had just finished reading the letter when the storm broke loose."

"She lost her way and could not make out any landmarks. When we spoke after she regained consciousness she told me that she not only took to heart my letter, but if my proposal was still in place, she would gladly accept my request for her hand. This can be confirmed with Doctor

Lyndon who was in the room as Elizabeth and I spoke. So, sir, I now inform you of my desire to marry your daughter. I understand that you will, obviously, withhold your final decision until you have a chance to speak with Elizabeth, but, please know, I refuse to be banned from the infirmary and her side. This is why my dear cousin, Anne, has prepared these rooms so that I may meet with others and yet be close to the infirmary at all times. I refuse to be any further away. I know that propriety would frown on my involvement in the care of Elizabeth, but I have never held much stock in what propriety dictates."

Mr. Bennet was shocked at not only Mr. Darcy's declaration of love for his beloved daughter, but to learn of her accepting his hand. Mr. Darcy was correct in that he would hold off his final decision of approval until Elizabeth could confirm her acceptance. "Mr. Darcy, I am taken aback by this information. I ask for some time for this to all sink in. As for banning you from her side, if you show me that your intentions are honorable, I will have no difficulties with you being of assistance to Elizabeth as she recovers from this event. And so you are aware, she is a very strong young lady. She has never allowed any illness or injury to keep her down for long. I have no doubt that she will be well in no time."

"It is my deepest hope and prayer that you are correct. I will now take you to see her, if you would like."

"I would be grateful if you did sir. After that if you could have someone show us to my cousin's parsonage so that we might refresh."

"My cousin has extended the invitation to all of you to stay here at the house. She would not dream of your being so far from your daughter during her recovery. Her housekeeper has had rooms prepared for all of you and I will ask that baths be drawn and ready for you in an hour if that meets with your approval. Would you care to eat first or after freshening up?"

"After would be fine, and I would be quite grateful for both the baths and your cousin's generosity. I do wish to remain close by my Lizzy, as I know Mary and Jane would wish as well. Please know how truly grateful I am to you as well Mr. Darcy. From all that you have told us, you have done everything possible for Lizzy."

"Mr. Bennet, I only wish there was more I could do for her. As I have said, I truly do love her and wish to marry her. I would move heaven and earth if I could protect her. And if there is anything else she needs, all that is necessary is for me to learn of the need and the need will be fulfilled."

Darcy escorted the Bennets inside the infirmary only to hear Jane and Mary gasp. Mr. Bennet appeared to age in a matter of moments. Lying on the bed, her wounds wrapped in bandages, and the raging fever coursing through her, Elizabeth appeared so frail and broken. Darcy instantly picked up a cloth from her forehead and rinsed it in the basin of cold water and replaced it on her forehead. It was quite obvious to Mr. Bennet that this was a behavior which Darcy had performed many times in the past few days. He watched the tenderness of Darcy's touch, his concerned look as he viewed the fever riddled body of the woman he claimed to love.

Doctor Lyndon returned to the room with another chunk of ice. Darcy introduced the doctor to the Bennets. "Doctor, how is my daughter?"

"I wish there was better news to give you sir. I am sure that you were made aware of her injuries from the fall. Her fever began yesterday and has continued to climb. It is dangerously high at this time. We have been trying to cool her down with cool cloths and pieces of ice. So far, we have not been successful. I feel it is time to take a drastic step. Mr. Bennet, Mr. Darcy, I feel that the only hope of breaking the hold that the fever has on Miss Elizabeth is to subject her to an ice bath."

"And what does that entail, Doctor? What will this do for my daughter?"

"We will place Miss Elizabeth in the bathing tub and completely cover her with ice. She would remain in this until the fever breaks. There is danger of doing this though."

"What is the danger?" Darcy asked nervously.

"Sir, the drastic change to the body temperature could cause her heart to stop. But, if it is not done, the fever will kill her. Either way she is in danger of loosing her life. I will allow you to discuss the options between you, but know that we must do make a decision as soon as possible."

Jane and Mary decided to step out of the room to allow the two men who loved Elizabeth to decide her fate. Outside the door of the infirmary, Jane began to sob for her sister. Bingley was nearby and came forward to place a comforting arm around Jane's shoulders and lead her to a nearby bench. "Mr. Bingley, she looks so poorly. The doctor spoke of her near death. Not Lizzy. I could not bear to loose my dear sister." Jane continued to sob. Mary stood near the infirmary door shaking as she tried desperately to contain her sorrow.

Fitzwilliam was nearby and was moved by the sorrow that was apparent in Mary's expression. He moved towards her, asking if he could be of assistance to her. "I thank you sir. It is just so difficult to realize that it is really Lizzy lying there on that bed."

"I understand. I was with my cousin when we found her. Darcy and I were the ones to climb down on ropes to bring her back up. He has been by her side day and night. Only when Mrs. Collins or Anne volunteer to sit by her side while he takes a few moments to eat or rest does he leave her side. Anne had this room here cleared out and furniture brought in so Darcy would have a room close by. He takes his meals in this sitting room, takes short naps here as well. He has not laid his head on his pillow since the accident."

"Mr. Darcy proposed to Elizabeth and she has accepted him?"

"My cousin did indeed propose to her and after we brought her here and she regained consciousness she accepted his proposal. He is very devoted to her. I have never seen him like this before. I fear not only for her safety but for his if he were to lose her after finally finding her."

"Lizzy has always been strong. We have to believe that she is meant to survive and share her life with Mr. Darcy. We must hold on to our faith that she will survive."

Fitzwilliam took a hold of Mary's hand and led her into the sitting room, leaving the door open to the hallway. "Would you like something to drink? A glass of wine to calm your nerves?"

Mary looked at Fitzwilliam with confusion. "I am sorry sir, I forgot to introduce myself to you. I do not even know your name. I am Mary Bennet, the middle daughter, next after Elizabeth. My sister who was sitting with Mr. Bingley is our eldest sister, Jane."

"Miss Mary, may I present myself to you? I am Colonel Richard Fitzwilliam, Darcy's cousin. I am the second son of Lord and Lady Matlock, of Derbyshire. This estate belongs to my cousin, Lady Anne de Bourgh."

"Lady Anne? Mr. Collins always claimed his patroness to be a Lady Catherine."

"I will explain this to you later, as it is a long story. My cousin is legally the heir of Rosings, but she had allowed her mother to continue to rule. That was, until Lady Catherine tried to interfere with Darcy bringing Elizabeth here for medical aid. When Lady Catherine continued to make demands of Darcy, refusing to listen to him, Anne decided to refuse allowing her mother's rule. Anne is now in charge of Rosings. My parents are on their way to be of assistance to both of my cousins. Assisting Anne with the legal paperwork, as she takes charge of the estate, and Darcy, as he awaits Elizabeth's recovery."

"It appears that there have been many activities occurring here."

"It has not been dull by any means. At this point, there has been more commotion going on than I have seen in war. I can only hope for a peaceful and happy ending to all of these events."

"Dear me, that is very hectic.   And how is your aunt accepting her fate?"

"Not well, though she has remained in her suite and not bothered any of us."

"Maybe that is a blessing from what you have said and the description of her we were given by Mr. Collins."

Fitzwilliam smiled and laughed. "At that Miss Mary, you are correct."

Chapter 7

The door of the infirmary opened and the men stepped out. Mary and Jane quickly came to their father. Jane embraced her father as she wept. "What have you decided for Lizzy?"

"Mr. Darcy and I have agreed on the ice bath. The doctor is sending for the ice as we speak. Mr. Darcy and Doctor Lyndon will be with her. Do either of you girls desire to be with Lizzy during this? I know that I would not be able to be by her side watching this. I will stay here in Mr. Darcy's sitting room. Charlotte Collins is available to attend Lizzy, if you girls do not feel you are capable of doing so."

"Papa, I do not know about Jane, but I would appreciate the chance to be at Lizzy's side and give her any aid I can. Even if it is only giving her my strength and words of comfort."

"Mary, as much as I wish I could be at our sister's side, after seeing her lying there so still, I do not feel strong enough to be in there during this treatment. I will stay with Papa."

Bingley acknowledged Jane's feelings. "I will remain with you Mr. Bennet and Jane. If I may be of comfort to you, you need only ask."

Darcy opened the door of the infirmary to inquire as to who was coming into the bathing chamber to aid Elizabeth. Mary stepped forward and entered the room. Charlotte was called for from the parsonage, and she arrived just as the ice did.

Darcy carefully lifted Elizabeth from the bed and carried her in to the bathing chamber. He placed her into the empty tub, leaning her head back against a pillow he held against the end of the tub. Darcy continued to hold her there, as the others placed chunks of ice on and around Elizabeth's body. Darcy was charged with the duty of holding Elizabeth's head and neck in place in case she was to come to during this procedure. If she was to jerk as she was revived, she could injure herself even further.

By being beside Elizabeth's head, Darcy was able to whisper words of encouragement to her. He pleaded with her to remain with him, not to leave him now that he had found her. Mary found tears streaming from her eyes as she listened to this man who had been believed to be so somber and taciturn, showing Elizabeth such love and devotion.

Each minute ticked by slowly, feeling like an hour. Each breath Elizabeth took was watched with agony by the four people in the room with her. Nearly two hours after the ice had been placed on her, Elizabeth woke with extreme shivers running through her body. The fever had broken.

Tears flowed freely down Darcy's face as he gave thanks for Elizabeth's return to them. After the ice was removed from on top of Elizabeth, Darcy picked her up from the tub and laid her on a table nearby in the bathing chamber. The men stepped from the room to allow Charlotte and Mary to assist Elizabeth to dry off and place fresh clothes on her. Darcy then returned and carried his beloved to her bed in the infirmary, which had fresh linens on it. After placing her head on the pillow and pulling the coverlet over her body, Darcy stepped to the door and opened it.

"Mr. Bennet, Miss Bennet, everyone. The fever has broken. She is doing much better. She is awake."

Mr. Bennet and Jane came quickly to Elizabeth's bedside, with Bingley and Fitzwilliam standing near the door.

"Lizzy, thank the heavens you have returned to us. My dear sister, you are never to scare us like this again." Jane took hold of one of Elizabeth's hands.

Mr. Bennet took hold of the other hand. "I agree with your sister's sentiment. I will not tolerate you being so ill ever again.

Do you understand me? You are my beloved daughter, and loved by all of us. We will not tolerate the possibility of loosing you."

Elizabeth was able to give her family a weak smile. She had returned to them. She would live. Darcy made to step out of the room and allow Elizabeth time with her family when suddenly she called out to him.

"Please do not leave now William." Elizabeth pleaded with him.

"Dearest, I was only allowing your family some time with you. I have no intention of leaving you."

This calmed the worried look on her face. "Papa, I do not know if you were made aware, but I have accepted Mr. Darcy's request for my hand in marriage. I pray that you will approve of my choice. He is the very best of men."

Mr. Bennet smiled at his daughter. "I was told of the events and was also told that Mr. Darcy did not expect me to give my final decision until I had confirmed it with you. So I am understanding that you do indeed wish to marry Mr. Darcy."

"I do wish to marry William. As I said, he is the very best of men." Just then Elizabeth noticed Bingley in the back of the room. "Mr. Bingley, it is good to see you again."

"As it is you Miss Elizabeth. I arrived as soon as I could after being sent an express from your future husband. He requested me to come quickly. And he has given me a second chance to learn more about your elder sister. So even though I do not wish you to be ill and I am truly grateful for your recovery, I cannot be sorry to come and be here during this time. You have given me a great gift."

Elizabeth looked at Darcy with tears in her eyes. "Did you do what I think you did?"

Nodding, Darcy stepped forward. "I did indeed dearest. I have spoken with Bingley about it all."

"William, my love, thank you so very much."

"I was wrong, and you were correct. I just rectified the problem which I created." This brought looks of confusion from Elizabeth's family. "We will explain later what we mean. Just know for now that William did something wonderful to aid our family."

Doctor Lyndon returned to the room and insisted the majority of the group leave to allow Elizabeth to get some much needed rest. "Mr. Bennet, if you would like to have some time alone with Elizabeth, I will step out and be across the hall."

"I would appreciate that Mr. Darcy. From the looks of it, you need not stay away very long as I know my daughter will desire you by her side soon."

Darcy smiled. "I will request some broth and breads be brought. Elizabeth, you will need nourishment to recover."

"We are not even married and he is already a mother hen." She smiled openly to Darcy. "Perhaps some herbal tea to help settle my stomach as well. Mary, do you remember how to make the blend that I have always found soothing?"

"As you entrusted your secret to me years ago, I do indeed know how to make it." Mary laughed. Turning towards Fitzwilliam and Bingley she continued. "I was sworn to secrecy years ago. I do not remember where Lizzy learned this recipe, but I have found it soothing when I have used it as well."

Darcy and Mary stepped into the hallway to make their requests to the servants. Elizabeth looked at Jane and smiled. "Now is your chance to become reacquainted with Mr. Bingley. Take hold of this chance and do not allow anyone else to stand in your way." Seeing Bingley in the hallway waiting to be there for Jane, Elizabeth pulled her sister closer. "I have it on good authority that Bingley truly loves you. I know that you love him as well. Explore your wishes and spend time with him. Now go on. Shoo."

Jane laughed at her sister's silliness. "As you command, my dear sister. As you command."

The others had stepped out of the room and allowed Mr. Bennet some time alone with his daughter. "Lizzy, I am so pleased to see you recovered so. My heart was torn apart when the doctor informed us of your very grave condition. Life would not have been tolerable if you were no longer here with us. Do not attempt this again."

"Papa, you mean you do not wish to find me ill and unable to even inform you that I have accepted a man's hand in marriage?" She was trying desperately to lighten the mood.

"It was a very unusual way to learn of your daughter's plan to wed. Not one I would relish enduring again any time soon. Now, tell me, are you truly in love with Mr. Darcy? Do not confuse love for thankfulness for what he has done for you."

"I had made my decision to accept William before the storm struck and before William rescued me. My feelings for him are genuine. They are not from some mistaken feeling of honor towards him for his rescue. It is for his being the man he is. A very kind and loving man who cares deeply for me. It will be a very wonderful marriage Papa."

"I will give you my blessing then. I could not have tolerated giving you away to anyone less worthy. I love you Lizzy. I will welcome your Mr. Darcy for his devotion to you."

A knock on the door announced Darcy's return. He came carrying a tray containing broth, breads, tea, and fruits.

"Do you expect me to be able to consume all of that?"

Darcy smiled at her question. "It was made known to me that I had not eaten all day as I was either with you or across the hall speaking with family or friends. So I decided to join you in our first meal together since we became engaged."

"I am marrying a romantic." Elizabeth laughed and then winced at a twinge of pain in her side.

"Are you well, dearest? Should I send for Doctor Lyndon?"

"Just a slight pain when I laughed. Nothing to worry over. Do not fret William. You fall off a hill and see if you have aches and pains anywhere in your body." Darcy laughed at his over reacting.

"Mr. Bennet, there is enough here for you as well. I even brought an extra tea cup for you."

"I would appreciate a cup of tea, thank you. And since you are to become my son, you may call me Bennet or Father."

"Many thanks sir. Please call me William. Here is your cup." Darcy handed him a cup. "Now young lady, we need to see how much we can get you to eat to help you build up your strength. It has been three days since you have had any real nourishment."

"It is obvious that I would be spoiled if my future husband had his way."

"Do you mean the chair from Egypt to carry royalty that I ordered will not be useful?"

This made the three of them laugh. "Hearing your laughter again does my heart good. I feared I would not ever have the pleasure. Elizabeth, you must promise me to start each day of our life together with a laugh."

"If you insist William. Mainly so that I may have the privilege of seeing your dimples when you smile."

"Mr. Bennet, I feel your daughter is relapsing. I have no dimples. Have you ever seen any signs of a dimple on my face?" He tried hard to contain a laugh.

"Why come to think of it sir, I have not seen such a thing on your face. But then again, until now, I have not witnessed seeing a smile on your face or hearing you laugh."

"Primarily due to no reason to smile. I had not yet been blessed with the honor of your daughter's hand."

"I can understand how she can create a need to smile in most people."

Chapter 8

Elizabeth was able to drink a cup of broth, and eat some fruit and bread. It was not much in comparison to what most people would eat, but the fever and injuries had decreased her appetite. By the time she finished, she was extremely tired.

Darcy gave Elizabeth a kiss on the head and wished her a peaceful sleep. He would be across the hall if she needed him. Mr. Bennet then kissed his daughter as well and left her to her sleep. A nurse, who had been hired to assist in Elizabeth's care, came to sit near her patient.

As the two men stepped out into the hallway, Darcy found his sister wrapping her arms around his waist. "Georgiana, when did you arrive?" He looked up to see his aunt and uncle had apparently arrived with his sister. "It is good to see you both as well." He said as he shook his uncle's hand and embraced his aunt. "Have you all been brought up to speed on what has occurred here this week?"

Lord Matlock looked at his nephew and shook his head. "Only what Richard wrote to us. We just barely arrived as you were coming from the room."

"Let us step into the sitting room here." Darcy motioned to the room across from the infirmary. Lord Matlock frowned at this. "When did this turn into a sitting room? I thought it was a storage area."

"It was Uncle Henry." Anne stepped towards the group. "We converted it for Cousin William when he refused to stray any further from the infirmary. It had been a suite at one time I was told."

"I seem to vaguely remember that. Yes, let us step in there so we can be brought up to current events."

After everyone was situated in the sitting room, Darcy began making introductions. The discussion began with the accident, and then proceeded into Lady Catherine's behavior and Anne's decision to replace her mother. Darcy further explained the continuing health problems which Elizabeth had struggled with and of the ice bath which broke the fever. Darcy was quite pleased with the progress which Elizabeth made by partaking in the food Darcy had brought for her to eat.

Lord and Lady Matlock were amazed at the changes in their family. First Darcy openly admitting to being in love with a young lady of inferior birth, then standing his ground with Lady Catherine and Anne coming forward to stand against her mother as well. Georgiana had received letters from her brother, and had learned of his growing attraction to Elizabeth, so this did not surprise her. Darcy standing up to their aunt was shocking though. She sat next to her brother, holding his hand as he spoke. Georgiana felt his grip tighten when his fears were spoken of. She attempted to reassure him with light squeezes.

Anne spoke of her confrontation with her mother and her plans for Rosings. Lord Matlock informed her that all she needed to do was to notify their attorney and sign some papers to take her rightful and legal place as Mistress of Rosings. Lord

Matlock would send an express to the attorney and request that he send someone to Rosings with the papers. Lady Matlock was to take the lead on opening the Dowager House for Lady Catherine. This would be a joyous treat for Elaine Fitzwilliam, as she had despised her sister in law's treatment of others, especially her own family members. To learn that her own son stood with his cousins against Catherine's tirade was pleasing as well.

Lord Matlock turned to Mr. Bennet. "Sir, I have forgotten to inquire as to your feelings towards the marriage. Are you in support of it or against it?"

"As I saw no signs of a partiality on either side while Darcy was in Hertfordshire, I held out my decision of approval until I could speak with my daughter. Not only was I told by my daughter of her desire to marry Darcy, but was witness to the warmth and devotion which has developed between them. It will not be a marriage of convenience. They truly love each other. And this is the only type of marriage I would have approved for my beloved daughter."

"Please pardon me as I ask you these next questions. I do not wish to offend you, but I too am only looking out for a dearly loved family member."

Mr. Bennet smiled and nodded. "I will answer you honestly sir and find no offense in protecting your loved ones. I understand such devotion."

"What is your daughter's circumstance? What of your family and your family connections? What does she have to offer to such a marriage?"

"Sir, I am a country gentleman, my estate is Longbourn in Hertfordshire. It has been in my family since my great, great grandfather. There is an entailment in place, and as I have no sons, the estate will pass to my distant cousin, Mr. Collins, who is the parson here at Hunsford. I have five daughters, with my eldest three here at this home. This is my eldest, Jane. Elizabeth is next, followed by Mary. My youngest two daughters are at home with their mother. They are silly young girls who need to have more restraint. They are not as precious as my eldest three. Each of my daughters will have only fifty pounds at my death, along with their own charms to promote themselves. These three here are far from being mercenary in their desires to wed, they are no fortune hunters. Elizabeth herself turned down Mr. Collins when he came to Longbourn to visit and made her an offer. Marriage to him would have made her family secured upon my death, as her mother and sisters would have a home upon my demise. But there was no attraction and even greater, no love or respect for this man. Elizabeth refused and I supported her decision, though at the time we had no way of knowing if another offer would ever come. We had no way of knowing at that time of Darcy's interest, as he hid his feelings quite well. Elizabeth has been raised as the son I never had. She is well educated, with a superior wit and a thirst for reading. She prefers long walks out of doors and enjoying nature over silly things such as ribbons and lace. She is very devoted to her family and close friends."

"Might I add too, Bennet, that Elizabeth is beautiful. She has chestnut brown hair, brown eyes which sparkle with life. Her smile is to be experienced to understand. She challenges me, using her impertinence to make me look at my own way of evaluating others. I am a better person for having Elizabeth in my life."

Lord Matlock had tears running down his cheek as he listened to his nephew. "I am convinced that your feelings are true, Darcy. I will hold my final verdict on this attachment until I have a chance to meet Miss Elizabeth, but from what I have heard here, it is merely a formality. As you may have known, Darcy, your father charged me with the task of ensuring you choose a love match over a marriage of convenience. I am proud of you for preferring such an attachment. Now, after all that you have been through, I am sure that you could use a good night's sleep. Why do you not do just that while all of us are here to take turns watching over your betrothed?"

"I could use a few hours of sleep. I will be in the next room. Please do not hesitate to wake me if there is any change in Elizabeth's condition or if she needs me."

The others left the sitting room to allow Darcy to rest. Jane determined to take the first shift at her sister's side, followed by Mary, then Mr. Bennet, Lady Matlock, Georgiana, and even Anne. Bingley decided to situate himself outside on the bench while Jane was inside, incase Jane should need his strength. When Mary took her turn, Fitzwilliam felt the same desire to be ready to lend a shoulder if needed.

Fortunately, Elizabeth rested peacefully throughout the night.

Chapter 9

The following day Elizabeth had pain from her many injuries, though she was pleased to have her family at her side and enjoyed meeting Colonel Fitzwilliam's mother and Georgiana. She apologized to them for not being properly attired and in better shape to meet them. They were all impressed with this lady who had captured Darcy's heart.

Lord Matlock waited until the attorney's assistant arrived before approaching his sister. She was furious at being told she must leave her home and move to the dowager house. For Anne to stand up to her infuriated Lady Catherine, and then to have the rest of the family support her decisions further irritated the bitter woman.

"Catherine, you are well aware your desire for Darcy to marry your daughter was your dream, and our sister had no such dream for her son. You waited until after our sister was dead to begin your campaign to join the two estates. You and you alone were the only one who wished for this union.

You were told year after year that Darcy did not wish for this, Anne did not wish for this, Gerald was against your wish, I am against your wish, and no one with any wisdom would choose Anne for Darcy. They are not in love. I was given the task by our brother in law to ensure that Darcy chose his bride for love. So I would always stand in your way in your quest."

"Henry, it would be a wonderful match. Anne was made for Darcy, she is not only of the first circles, but would bring a title to the Darcy family name, and I would be allowed to remain at Rosings, as Darcy would not wish to live here over Pemberley. Anne's dowry would increase Pemberley as well."

"Catherine, your years of trying to force such a match are over. Darcy has made his choice. My wife has spoken briefly with Miss Elizabeth and finds her everything we have been told. We will be supporting Darcy's choice. We are also supporting Anne in her decision to step forward to take command of her inheritance. We will stay and help you with your move to the dowager house."

Lord Matlock stood and walked to the door. "Make no mistake, Sister, your days of demanding everyone to do as you wish are over. If you do anything to harm your daughter, Darcy, Miss Elizabeth or anyone else, I will speak to the attorney about cutting you out of your inheritance and possibly sending you to an institution as you obviously have not been thinking clearly for some time." He then walked out the door, leaving behind his sister with her mouth hanging open.

Darcy had not realized how tired he was. The past few days had drained him not only physically, but emotionally as well. When he woke, he was surprised to learn he had slept for more than twelve hours. He immediately went to check on Elizabeth, and finding she was sleeping, went back to his new rooms to bathe and clean up. Rogers was ready for his master, having ordered the bath drawn as soon as Darcy woke and set up the shaving supplies. He laid out clean clothes for Darcy to wear, as the past few days he had not put much concern to his appearance. First was the shave and a slight trim of Darcy's hair. Next was the bath. After the water was poured over his head to rinse him, Darcy stepped out to dry off. He then dressed and, after peering in to confirm Elizabeth still resting, ordered a tray of food brought to share with his betrothed. He picked up a book from his belongings in the sitting room and entered the infirmary to read as he waited for his love to wake.

"What has caught your attention so intensely Mr. Darcy?"

He looked up from his book to see the eyes of his betrothed open and watching him. "How long have you been watching me?" He smiled at Elizabeth and put his book down.

"Not too long, though I was enjoying seeing a look of joy in your eyes. What are you reading?"

"It is not the book which has placed joy in my life, though it is a very good book on a new method of farming which I wish to implement in the next planting season. It is better for the land and produces better crops. New techniques come up all the time, though I find this one to be a sound and viable method. And what are you smiling at Elizabeth?"

"I am smiling at you William. I am pleased to hear you speak of your estate so. My father does not take an active role in his estate so it does my heart good to see your devotion to yours. It makes me proud of you."

"I was taught to respect my estate and the people who work it, for without them, Pemberley would be nothing. I have a great respect for my staff and tenants."

"I am very proud of you. I agree with your view. Now, sir, how are you fairing today? You appear much better rested, and even well attired. Though I do admit that I found you dressed in only your shirt tail and breeches to be quite fetching."

"My dear, as ill as you were and you were thinking of how fetching you found me in my attire? I am truly surprised."

"William, it was because of you and your caring that I survived. Of course I would wish to live after knowing what a truly wonderful man I am to marry. And knowing how attractive you are was also an enticement to live. My love, you have no notion of how pleased I am to have you by my side. Your love, devotion, caring, and desire to ignore propriety for my sake have made me realize just how fortunate I am to have accepted you. And I thank you for what you have done for my beloved sister. She has spoken to me of Mr. Bingley's return to her side, after you had requested him here and told him of your complicity in separating him from Jane. William, thank you. I can already see the return of joy in Jane's eyes. She truly loves Bingley, and I have a feeling that Bingley may fall in love with her."

"He already has. He has admitted as much to me. He will speak to your father after you are better. And we have another budding romance developing."

Elizabeth raised an eyebrow as she watched Darcy. "Who might that be, sir?"

"Mary has sparked a fire in Fitzwilliam's eyes. I think that her feelings may be of a similar spark. Aunt Elaine has also noticed and is encouraging the spark into a small flame, hoping for it to fully bloom." He had a smile on his face which showed a pair of beautiful dimples on his cheeks. Elizabeth knew that it was rare for anyone to see these dimples and she felt very privileged. "Ah, love is erupting at Rosings. How did your aunt handle all of this disruption in her home?"

"Actually, it is not her home. It is Anne's home, as it was willed to her, and became hers over two years ago. She had just allowed her mother to remain as she was. When my aunt insisted that you be removed to Longbourn immediately, I refused. My aunt became irate and demanded my marriage to Anne. As I stood up to her, Anne and Fitzwilliam came to stand at my side. Anne refused to allow your health to be jeopardized any further. She has even begun the process to have her mother removed to the dowager house."

"Anne has no desire to marry me, as her mother demands us to do. Uncle Henry also knows that my mother never desired any attachment between myself and

Anne. Fitzwilliam added his piece to the argument, telling my aunt of my father's request to my uncle to ensure I marry for love rather than consequence. My family is here, with the exception of Fitzwilliam's elder brother, Matthew. They are all pleased with my choice of a bride and are supporting our union. Of course your father and two of your sisters are here as well as Bingley. All are surprised yet pleased with the young lady who has stolen my heart."

Darcy lifted Elizabeth's hand to place a kiss in the palm of it. Elizabeth placed a hand lightly against his cheek. "I cannot tell you how I felt to wake, knowing of your love and kindness. Through all of this trial, I have discovered my heart and am pleased to place it in your gentle care. You truly are the very best of men. My dearest, may I beg of you some tea?"

"Of course. Are your hungry as well? When was the last time you ate?" Darcy pulled the cord which alerted the staff that assistance was requested.

"I ate breakfast with Jane and Georgiana. They were both here and brought me some more broth, eggs, and fruit. I knew if you were to find out that I had not eaten, you would not be pleased. I also wish to regain my strength so that we can start planning our life together. I like your sister very much. She is quite sweet, and very shy. I realize now that what I took for arrogance and pride was actually your shyness and inability to feel comfortable with others. You hide within yourself." Darcy nodded as he looked down to the floor. "But when I was lost, I am told you took charge of everything and even were the one to come down the hill to retrieve me. Once here, you also took charge. What was so different?"

"It was more important to deal with everyone and everything because my concern was for you. There was nothing else important and I was able to forget my shyness. Had you met me at Pemberley, you would have discovered my true self months ago. It is where I am most comfortable and able to be myself. Instead, you met me at my worst. With all of the eligible young ladies and their matchmaking mamas attempting to snare a prize, I revert inside myself. If I had not been the Master of Pemberley and caring for Georgiana, I would never have had to deal with society's rules. If I could have stayed on my estate forever, I would truly be pleased."

"I have much to learn about you. I have had so many misconceptions about you. Can you forgive me for calling you arrogant? Will you give me time to learn the real William?"

"I will give you the rest of our lives to know me. And there is no need to forgive you for calling me arrogant. In a way I was. I gave no thought as to your feelings, as I thought you would immediately accept my attentions. When you called me arrogant, my feelings were injured and I struck back at you for the injury. I only realized after leaving you how badly I bungled my approach. How could I expect you to accept me after my comments about your family being unfit? What a fool I was to say to you that your family was inferior. I am even more amazed that you not only read my letter but decided to forgive me and accept my proposal. You have truly given me a gift and I will cherish it always. I will ask you to bear with me as I will no doubt have times of reverting back inside my shy self in certain circumstances."

Elizabeth smiled at this man whom she was just beginning to know. "I will bear with you for the rest of our lives, so long as you allow me to tease you occasionally about said behavior."

"I will always allow you to coax me out of my shell with your wit. It is one of the things that made me fall in love with you."

A knock on the door announced the arrival of Mr. Bennet. "Well, my dear daughter, you are beginning to mend quite well. I am pleased. Mr. Darcy, you also look a great deal better today.

Amazing what some rest and care will do to improve one's appearance. Also, having someone to love can perform miracles."

Both Elizabeth and Darcy blushed. "Now, you two, let us discuss your decision to wed. What are your thoughts on the matter?"

Darcy looked at Elizabeth and then to her father. "I would prefer a short engagement. I do not perform well in public gatherings and I know from my time spent in Hertfordshire that Mrs. Bennet would enjoy nothing better than to parade me around to all the functions. I would prefer something quiet and personal, family and dear friends only."

Elizabeth squeezed his hand. "I do not relish Mama's enthusiastic response which I know she will have when she learns of our engagement. And I agree to your desire for a short engagement and a small, private wedding. Family and only the closest of friends. Of course we will have to wait for a while as it will be some time before I am able to walk down the aisle to you, William."

"Walk, ride up on a horse drawn carriage, carried in my arms, brought to me in a wheeled chair, it does not matter the method so long as in the end you are at my side when we take our vows. Having you become my wife is more important than how you arrive at my side."

"I agree with both of you. Elizabeth is correct in that she will need some time to recover before you wed. Her cuts need to mend, bruises fade and her body to regain its strength which was stolen by the raging fever. As to the broken leg and its time to heal. It could take several months for it to be completely healed. From what you have both stated, neither of you would enjoy such a delay. So I propose a compromise. In a month's time Lizzy should have all of her other physical injuries mended and will be feeling more like herself. We can take that time to address the method of transporting Elizabeth up the aisle to your waiting arms. Mrs. Bennet will be extremely disappointed as to your choice of a small wedding, as she is a devoted fan of the elaborate. I will do my best to control her from overwhelming the situation. Now, we must discuss where we will be holding the wedding. I would prefer to give my daughter away from my home. But it has many difficulties."

"How so Papa?"

"As William has pointed out, your mother will wish to parade you both around so she can crow about the wealth of her soon to be son in law. But if we are not in Longbourn, your mother will not have the upper hand of familiarity."

"I have a home in London and the estate in Derbyshire, named Pemberley. I would be pleased to host your family at either place. Or I know that Anne could be coaxed into hosting us here. She would love to be able to do so while forcing her mother to accept it."

Mr. Bennet thought for a few moments. "William, if we were to travel to

Pemberley, who would you have perform the wedding ceremony?"

"My god father is the Arch Bishop of Derby, near Matlock. I know that he is planning to travel later on to the continent. If he cannot do it, then I would turn to Mr. Morgan, who has the parish at Kympton. He is a very kind clergy whom I have a deep respect for."

"Did you say the Arch Bishop is to travel to the continent? When is he planning the trip?"

"I am not sure of his specific plans, though my uncle may know. I can call for him to join us."

"Please do. I think that this could be just the ticket for the solution."

Darcy pulled the cord to summon a servant. When the servant arrived he requested Lord Matlock to be requested to the infirmary. While waiting for Lord Matlock, Mr. Bennet informed the engaged couple of his plan.

When Lord Matlock knocked on the door, Darcy opened it and welcomed his uncle into the room. Lord Matlock had yet to meet Elizabeth himself as it would have been highly inappropriate for him to take turn at sitting beside her as his wife had done.

"Uncle Henry, may I take this moment to introduce you to my fiancé, Elizabeth

Bennet. Elizabeth, this is Henry Fitzwilliam, otherwise known as Lord Matlock."

Lord Matlock walked forward to offer his hand to her. "It is a pleasure to finally meet the woman who has captured my nephew's heart so completely. I never thought I would see the day he would fall so deeply into love. I am very happy for you both. Now, what is being discussed here? I assume it to be something to do with plans for your future."

"Lord Matlock, we are finding alternatives that will meet with the choices of our families. I know my wife well enough as does Lizzy, and it appears William, and she will wish for an elaborate wedding with everyone in the county invited. She will wish to crow over having a daughter marrying such a man as William. If we have the wedding from our home in

Hertfordshire, she will do as she wishes with no thought of the couple's wants. William was just telling me that if the wedding was held at Pemberley he would prefer the arch bishop to perform the service. He also said that the arch bishop is planning a trip to the continent soon. Do you know what his plan is?"

Lord Matlock looked at his nephew and then his betrothed. "My cousin is leaving in six weeks time for Belgium. He will then travel through out the continent for nearly three months time. What is the plan?"

"I was wondering if your cousin would be willing to tell a little white lie as a wedding gift to the couple."

A chuckle escaped Lord Matlock. "As he has done so years ago to keep not only William, but both of my sons from being taken out behind the barn and paddled for something they did, I am sure he will be willing to do so as a wedding gift. What do you have in mind?"

"If we have the wedding at Pemberley, the couple will have more control over the arrangements than they would at Longbourn or even in London. My wife would not know anyone there and would be out of her element. Lizzy and William have both declared the desire for a small wedding with only family and the very closest of friends. I have requested a month long engagement to allow Lizzy to recover most of her strength and allow most of her injuries to heal. We will address the method of her coming down the aisle at a later time as we know her broken leg will not be healed by then.

Now, if we were to ask your cousin to say that he would not dream of anyone else performing the service for his god child and where they do not wish to wait until he returns, we will have the wedding just before he prepares to leave. Would he be willing to come to the chapel at Pemberley for the service?"

"I will write a letter to him this very day. I am sure he will be pleased to come and perform this honor. He has always had a soft spot for this young man and I know he will join the ranks of family members who are happy for William finally finding love. We all know how shy William and Georgiana are and have spent years trying to protect them."

"Well, then, this is what I propose for a plan. I feel it is necessary for us to trespass on Lady Anne's hospitality for another week, if she is willing. Then we can move the party to Pemberley. I can send for my wife and other two daughters to meet us there in two weeks time. That will give Lizzy a week once we arrive to rest before her mother's arrival. Would you wish to have the Gardiners invited Lizzy? Your aunt grew up in Lambton, which is near Pemberley if I heard her correctly at Christmas. They would be able to find one of her friends to stay with in Lambton."

"It will not be necessary for them to stay anywhere other than at Pemberley. We have four and twenty bed chambers in the main house, as well as empty rooms in the servant house and a currently empty gamekeeper's house nearby. So, as you can see, we will have more than enough room for all of your family and my family, our closest friends and not come close to filling up Pemberley. I insist you invite the Gardiners to stay in the family wing at the main house. That is if you desire them being invited, Elizabeth."

"Aunt Madelyn and Uncle Edward are very dear to me, as are my four young cousins. I would dearly love to have them at our wedding. Aunt Phillips and her family are not as close to Jane and I, so it would not be as important to me for them to be invited. The only family you have left Papa is Mr. Collins. I suppose he and Charlotte should be invited. I do not relish his being there, but would like having Charlotte at my wedding."

"An invitation will then be extended to Mr. and Mrs. Collins my dearest."

"Well, then, gentlemen, I propose we allow Lizzy to rest some more and we can continue this discussion further at a later time. Lord Matlock, if you would be so kind as to write your cousin and ensure his cooperation, I would appreciate it. William, you should probably write to your housekeeper and prepare her for the upcoming event. I will begin the process of preparing Mrs. Bennet for the event." Mr. Bennet smiled at his daughter who was obviously fatigued. He leaned over and kissed her forehead. "Now Lizzy, be a good girl and get plenty of rest. I love you."

"I will do just that Papa. Thank you for all of your efforts." Elizabeth could hardly keep her eyes open by this time. "Lord Matlock, it is a pleasure to meet you. I know we will speak again later." A yawn escaped her as Darcy squeezed her hand. "Please, William, will you stay and read to me until I am asleep?"

"Of course I will. Let me show the men to the door and I will be pleased to read to you."

Chapter 10

Within half an hour, while holding on to Darcy's hand, Elizabeth was sleeping soundly. Darcy laid her hand on the bed as he stepped across the hall to the sitting room. He picked up his stationary items and prepared to write a very unusual letter that would undoubtedly shock his housekeeper. Mrs. Reynolds had been his family's housekeeper since Darcy was near four years of age. She was very devoted to both Darcy and his sister. He took a moment to consider what he would say to her. Finally he picked up his pen.

March 10, 1803

Mrs. Reynolds,

I have some news which will no doubt cause confusion and excitement at Pemberley. Georgiana and I will be coming home in nearly a week's time. I will send you another letter when I know the exact date. We will be arriving with guests as well. Now to tell you the most amazing tale.

As you were already aware, I spent last fall in Hertfordshire at the estate which Mr. Bingley had leased. What you did not know was that my interest was peaked after meeting a daughter of one of the local country gentlemen. The lady's name is Elizabeth Bennet.

Miss Elizabeth Bennet's cousin is my aunt's clergy at Hunsford, and I was surprised to discover her visiting her cousin and his wife when I arrived with Colonel Fitzwilliam for our annual visit.

The day my cousin and I were to leave to return to London, a severe storm struck with rain which made visibility impossible. Miss Elizabeth had been walking in the park near Rosings and as she finished reading a letter she had received, she was stuck in the storm. She lost her way and fell over the top of a hill on the property. We were unable to search for her until the storm relented the following day, after she lay broken in the storm for many hours. We brought her back to Rosings, where she has been in the care of the surgeon. When she became conscious, she accepted my proposal and is willing to give me her hand in marriage.

She then developed an extremely high fever which raged through her for two days. Fortunately, the fever broke after an ice bath. Elizabeth is now on the mend. She has a broken leg and cuts, abrasions and bruises from the fall, including a large gash on the side of her head which had to be stitched by the surgeon.

Elizabeth's father, Mr. Bennet, and has given us his blessing. We have decided on a wedding in one month's time. As both Elizabeth and I wish for a quiet and small event, Mr. Bennet has suggested we marry from Pemberley with the arch bishop presiding over the nuptials. This will allow us to keep the wedding the way we wish rather than the elegant and extravagant affair Mrs. Bennet would demand if we had the wedding from Elizabeth's home estate of Longbourn.

So, we will be having many guests over the next month arriving for our wedding. As we determine our plans, we will keep you informed. We are waiting to travel *until Elizabeth has had time to recover some of her strength.*

Now I have to ask for your assistance. I wish to have improvements made to the Mistress's chambers. I have included a list of items I feel need improvements or addressing. Nothing is to be overlooked, spare no expenses. I would also like for you to make arrangements with Mrs. Cantering to come to Pemberley to order Elizabeth's trousseau, preferably a week after we arrive, for I know that the trip will be tiring for Elizabeth. I wish for the doctor to be present and prepared to care for Elizabeth upon our arrival.

I am sending a letter to London to my attorney to have the marriage articles drawn up and to have the jewels which are stored in the family vault sent to Pemberley. When the jewels arrive, please lock them in the safe in my study. I will have Danny deliver them, for I trust him as my personal post rider.

I know that I am putting many issues on your shoulders to handle in my stead. I apologize to you now, for the inconvenience, and thank you for the perfect job I know you will do. You have never failed my family in all the years I have known you.

My great appreciation.

Fitzwilliam Darcy

Darcy made his list of improvements to be made to the Mistress's chambers, to have the infirmary prepared and notify Doctor Woodland of the situation as Darcy would prefer to have the doctor at Pemberley to check on his fiancé upon their arrival. He requested a wheeled chair be available for Elizabeth, as well as a cane for later on. He would have Lady Matlock send a list of items that will need to be ordered for Elizabeth as well.

The letter was finished and he requested a post rider to take the letter as well as the letter for his attorney for delivery. The first to be delivered was to Pemberley where the letter for the attorney would be given to Darcy's personal messenger Danny. Danny would wait in London for the items requested and then take them directly to Pemberley.

Darcy was walking back towards the infirmary door when one of the servants was bringing a tray of food and tea for Elizabeth. "I will take that. My thanks." As he took the tray and entered to see Elizabeth just waking. The servant stood in the hallway with a look of surprise that a gentleman would take the tray from her and then enter the room of an unmarried lady.

"So, did you have a pleasant rest?" Darcy asked as he placed the tray on a table near the bedside. "I am pleased to say I have completed all the business I needed to do and am now free to do your bidding."

"My dear Mr. Darcy, you are near giddy. I have never seen you so pleased." Elizabeth was moving slightly and discovered aches she did not earlier realize she had. "What pray tell has brought such joy to you?"

"Are you in pain? Do you need another dose of laudanum?" He was deeply concerned with her wincing.

"Nothing too painful, just discovering bruises I must have collected in the fall. Right now I think many of my bruises have

bruises. Now, back to my question. I
need to hear some joyful news."

"I have sent messages off to my
housekeeper and for my attorney. You
will love Mrs. Reynolds; she has known me
since I was four years old and has been
like a grandmother figure for me. I asked
her to prepare Pemberley for the great
event. This includes some changes to the
Mistress's suite, and to have the modiste
prepare to come to Pemberley after you
have had your first week there to recover
from the journey."

"I was not sure if you would wish to use
the infirmary when we first arrive, as you
will still be recovering. So it will be ready if
you prefer it over having to be brought
up and down to one of the guest rooms.
Unless you would prefer to move directly
into your suite. I would be sure that the

adjoining door to my suite was locked and your father could hold the key. It is your choice to make. I have also requested a wheeled chair for your convenience. I felt that it would give you a little more freedom rather than having to be carried at all times. Though I will have you know that I am very willing to carry you at anytime you wish. I just do not wish to overwhelm you. Oh, I am doing all of this so very poorly. I have been making arrangements without asking any questions of what you would prefer. I have made so many mistakes, I am sure of it."

Darcy stood and began to walk towards the door. "William, I require your assistance immediately."

He turned around quickly, concerned over her welfare. "What is wrong my dear?"

"I require my fiancé to sit beside me so that we might discuss the plans." Darcy smiled and walked back over to the chair beside the bed. "Now, first I think that you need to know why I changed my decision and agreed to marry you."

"I have been so happy that I was afraid to ruin it by asking questions."

"I had just finished reading the letter you wrote when the storm struck. At first I thought the storm would be over quickly so I did not hurry. I have walked in rain before and it does not bother me. But the storm did not let up and I could not see where I was going. I should have found somewhere to hide out, but I foolishly thought I was near the parsonage. Suddenly I found there was no earth under my feet and I went tumbling down. As I lay on the ground, to take my mind off the pain I was feeling, I began to go over your letter in my mind."

Elizabeth took a sip of water before continuing. "I went over and over your words, and how you opened yourself up and trusted me with the information about Georgiana. I realized the truth in your opinion of Jane's feelings, as she does not show them openly. And I knew I could speak with you about that topic, if I were to see you again. I realized the ways I had been wrong towards you and I did not have the strength to open myself up as you did in your letter. William, your letter showed a very deep part of your heart. A part of you which was very vulnerable. I could either decide to respect your giving me such a precious gift or I could forget it and forget you. I chose the first. The longer I lay there, the more I hoped that I would have a chance to see you again, to tell you how I appreciated your gift to me."

She reached up her hand to wipe away the tears streaming down her cheek. "Then I could have sworn that you were there with me at the bottom of the hill, holding me close. I knew that if I was dreaming of you being there with me, holding me so closely and lovingly, then I must have tender feelings for you which I had not allowed to surface. So I decided to allow my heart decide and when I saw you here beside me, I knew that my heart was leading me to you."

"Elizabeth, you were not dreaming of me at the bottom of the hill. I was there.

Fitzwilliam and I climbed down on ropes, secured you to a stretcher, and brought you back up the hill and to here."

"William, you could have been injured. What where you thinking?"

"I was thinking of the woman I loved dearly being injured and how I would not allow anything to stop me from reaching you. Fitzwilliam had to hold me back until better ropes could be brought as well as a stretcher. Standing at the top of the hill and seeing you lying there so still, not knowing if you were alive, my heart stopped beating. It only started beating again when I felt you breathing as I held you in my arms."

"When I woke here in this room with your arms around me, I knew I was where I belonged. I was home in your arms. I admit that there will be issues we need to discuss and work through, but I love seeing your excitement as you make these plans to make me happy. You have given Mr. Bingley and Jane another chance, and have been by my side through the worst moments of my life. How could I not wish to enjoy the greatest moments of my life with you?"

"So now I wish for you to tell me your opinions of what I told you of the letter I wrote to my housekeeper."

Elizabeth thought for a moment. "As I am not sure how I will feel when we arrive at Pemberley, I think you were wise to have the infirmary prepared. I hope I will not need it, but I also know that I am in a very tender stage of my recovery. I appreciate your request for a week at Pemberley before the modiste comes and all of the craziness begins with clothing designed and made, fittings, and more. You were very kind in giving me a chance to catch my breath when we first arrive. The wheeled chair will indeed give me some independence, but I will also appreciate the feel of your strong arms holding me near you. Now, what did your letter to your attorney have to deal with?"

Darcy leaned forward, resting his forehead on the top of her head gently. "I requested the marriage articles be prepared and the attorney to bring them to Pemberley for your father to review. I also requested some items removed from my vault and taken to Pemberley, but you will learn more of that when we arrive there."

"William, I feel so very blessed. Now, tell me how your aunt is handling all of this? Is Anne pleased with her decision?"

"Aunt Catherine is in the process of moving to the dowager house. She is not pleased and yet has kept very silent through it all. I have never been in her presence before and heard not a word. Uncle Henry and Aunt Elaine have made it quite clear that she is not to interfere in our plans or our lives. They are with her right now moving her. Anne is quite pleased and anxious at the same time. Fitzwilliam, Uncle Henry, Aunt Elaine, and I will help her over the next week, and they will stay on until the week before the wedding when they all plan to come to Pemberley. All with the exception of Aunt Catherine that is."

"I am so very sorry for causing so much difficulty for your family."

"Elizabeth, Aunt Catherine was leading to this moment for years and it was just a matter of time. It is all her doing, not yours. And you have actually aided Anne in taking control of her heritage. So thank you for that. Because of you she is stepping into the role she was born to take." Darcy held Elizabeth's hand and gave it a squeeze. "Now, dearest, you need to eat some of this food. I will stay here and read to you if you wish."

"I wish to see you eat as well. I cannot have you take ill or become injured, it would break my heart. So, let us both enjoy this tray of delicious morsels. And look, they even prepared for you as they sent a second cup." Elizabeth reached out her hand and placed it on the side of

Darcy's face. "Thank you, William. Thank you for giving me my life."

"Our life, my dear Elizabeth. It is now to be our life together."

Mr. Bennet sat down to write the letter to his wife. He decided at first to tell her of Lizzy's accident and then of her engagement to Mr. Darcy. He decided to tell her that for the time being, due to their daughter's fragile health, it was best for Rosings to remain calm and quiet. He would notify her when they planned to move from Rosings, though he did not inform her of the plans to move to Pemberley rather than Longbourn. Mr. Bennet repeatedly wrote in the letter that because of Elizabeth's health, a wedding date had not been fixed as it could be months before she was well enough to have the service. He also made references in his letter to Bingley being at Rosings and Jane spending time with him as they wait on word of Elizabeth. Mr. Bennet knew that this information would send his wife into pure delight. He repeated several times that Mrs. Bennet was not to begin making plans until Elizabeth was able to be consulted.

He then walked down the hall to leave the letter to be posted to Longbourn. He saw out of the window as Jane and Bingley walked by, taking in the out of doors. Mr. Bennet knew that Mary was reading in the front drawing room while she waited for Fitzwilliam to return to the house. The two of them had begun a friendship and it was bringing Mary out of her shell. After placing the envelope on the tray for posting, Mr. Bennet joined

Mary in the drawing room. "So, Mary, what are you reading there?"

"I was reading a book which Colonel Fitzwilliam recommended on some of the battles which had been waged in the past five years. When I asked him about some battles, he recommended the book and stated he would discuss it with me when he returned. He asked me if I wished to take a walk on the grounds tomorrow with him. I have accepted, if you approve Papa."

"I have faith in the Colonel being an honorable gentleman and feel that I may trust him to protect you on your walk. I give you my approval. Now, how do you feel about Lizzy's turn of events?"

"I am pleased. Pleased that she will survive what could have been a fatal accident and a fatal fever. And very pleased that she has found William to share her life with. It is very obvious how deeply they feel towards each other. I can only hope that one day I will find the same kind of love with someone myself."

"I hope that for all of my daughters. It appears as if Mr. Bingley has returned to showing his attentions to our Jane as well. There must be something magical in these waters which encourage young people to love. Or it could be that with your mother being absent from Rosing, you girls are able to relax and follow your hearts."

"I know that I have felt more at ease not having Mama here with her screeching. She would be floating with Lizzy marrying William, Jane and Mr. Bingley rekindling their feelings, and my spending time with

Colonel Fitzwilliam. Only problem is that there are no other men for Kitty and Lydia here. And I am quite pleased to have this time to know the Colonel before Kitty and Lydia meet him and squeal over his red coat."

"It is a very wise decision, my dear. And, Mary, may I add that I am very pleased to see you as you interact with people here. You have grown immensely in the past few days." Mr. Bennet walked over and embraced his middle daughter. "I am very proud of you Mary. Though I have often stated that Lizzy is my favorite, and your mother has always commented on Jane's beauty and Lydia's exuberance, I find you one of the finest young ladies I know. No father could be prouder."

Mary had tears falling down her cheeks as she returned her father's embrace. "Papa, thank you so much. I love you."

Just then, Fitzwilliam entered the room in search of Mary. Seeing her embracing her father with tears flowing, Fitzwilliam feared the worse. "Has something happened? Is Miss Elizabeth taken a turn for the worse?" He stepped forward towards Mary looking into her eyes for the answers to his questions.

"Oh, no, Colonel. My father and I were just speaking and I became nostalgic. Please forgive me, I must look a mess. I will be right back, I wish to freshen up." Mary gave her father another quick embrace and squeezed Fitzwilliam's hand before hurrying up the stairs to her room.

"Have no fears, Colonel. Mary is learning to step out from the shadow of her sisters and find her own worth. She is a very precious young lady and I was just informing her of how proud I am of her. With sisters such as Lizzy and Jane, as well as two younger and very silly sisters who are still at home and have no control over their behavior, Mary has been the quiet daughter in the shadow. I have sometimes forgotten to show her how dearly I love her."

"Mr. Bennet, I would like to ask if I may court Mary. I find her refreshing and appealing. I would like to spend more time getting to know her."

"Colonel, I would be honored to allow you to court my daughter."

The two men shook hands and smiled. Mary returned a few moments later and she left to go out of doors for a walk with Fitzwilliam.

Mr. Bennet walked down the hall to check on Elizabeth. She had been asleep when he checked in on her earlier in the afternoon. He knocked softly on the door and then quietly opened the door far enough to peer inside. The sight was incredible. Elizabeth was asleep on the bed with William asleep, seated on the floor with his head resting on the bed next to Elizabeth. She had evidently discovered him asleep, as her hand rested with her fingers tangled in his hair. Mr. Bennet knew that she was in love with this man. He could tell that he loved her as well. He wanted to spend a little time to discover just when Elizabeth realized her feelings for this man and why.

As Mr. Bennet stepped back and prepared to shut the door, he felt a hand touch his shoulder. He turned his head to see Lord Matlock standing there, peering into the same view as Mr. Bennet was witnessing. There was a smile gracing the face of Darcy's uncle.

The door was closed and Lord Matlock asked Mr. Bennet to join him in the study.

"Well, sir, these past few days have been a whirlwind. Let us take a little while to get to know each other, as we will be spending a great deal of time in the future together. If you have any questions, I ask you to feel free speak your mind."

"Lord Matlock, I would enjoy that."

"Please, call me Henry. Any father who has raised daughters who so completely capture the hearts of not only my nephew, but it appears my younger son, well, we should be on first name basis instead of bloody titles, do you not agree?"

"Completely, Henry. And I am Thomas. Yes, your son approached me just a short time ago and requested my permission to court my Mary. I must ask, what has your niece put in the water here to make such besotted fools of these three young men?"

"I need to ask Anne about that, as we could stand to put some in the water for my elder son and heir. He has yet to find a wife. Seems that Richard will be the first to reach the alter, and he will enjoy rubbing his brother's nose in that fact. Matthew has always enjoyed all his 'firsts' over Richard."

"Has Richard decided what he would like to do in his future? Does he plan to remain in the regulars?"

"Now that he is showing an interest in marrying and settling down, I need to have a chat with Richard. Unbeknownst to either of my sons, I set up a 'dowry' of sorts to be given to the bride of Richard's choice. This will allow him to choose any woman he chooses rather than settle for a marriage of convenience. I wish for my sons to have a loving marriage and home life. I have been very happily married to Elaine and wish the same for my sons. William's father set up a similar situation for his future bride. William is not aware of this yet. If I may, could I ask for you to be with me this evening when I inform both William and Richard of their inheritance. I would be grateful for your counsel with them."

"I would be honored Henry. This is incredible information and a very generous gift for each young man. To allow them to choose a woman from any circle of society for love, and yet give the unknown woman such a gift of making her an equal with the women of high society with said dowry, this is such a great honor. She would not be looked down upon by the cats and their matchmaking mamas because of her humble circumstances."

"Gerald Darcy and my sister Anne were truly and deeply in love. In our circle, that is a rare situation. Fortunately Anne and I both had love matches. Our sister Catherine did not. And from what you have heard while you have been here, but also from your cousin Mr. Collins, you must be well aware of the fact that Catherine did not have a happy life. But she chose title and prestige rather than felicity in marriage. She now reaps what she has sown over the years. Now, Gerald left in my safe keeping a letter for William for when he began to show an interest in any woman. It speaks of the inheritance for his bride. As this involves your daughter you should be there for the conversation. And being that it is another of your daughters involved with Richard, you have an interest there as well."

"Will you tell me more about William? We knew him briefly when he stayed at Netherfield Hall last fall. It is the estate which Bingley was leasing. No one was able to figure William out, as he was quite quiet and seemed taciturn. And yet you just witnessed such kindness and sweetness with my daughter."

"William has always been very tender where his heart is involved. But he has had several stumbling blocks which have kept him the man you have seen before. His mother died with Georgiana's birth. Anne had lost her previous child and was still frail when she became with child with Georgiana. Her death took a drastic hold on William and Gerald's lives. Also, there was a young man whom grew up with William, as his father was Gerald's steward. Mr. Wickham was a cunning con artist, very wild. William has spent a lifetime paying for Gerald's kindness to

Mr. Wickham. He is a man who has ruined many young ladies, cheated at cards, and run up many debts with local merchants."

"Did you say Wickham? George Wickham? He has been at my home several times as he is in the militia quartered in Meryton. My younger daughters have been quite fond of him."

"I warn you, send word to your daughters and wife informing them of Wickham's behaviors. No one is safe around him, especially innocent young girls."

"I will do just that. Thank you."

"William has always been a quiet child and young man. He keeps his feelings very close. To see his obvious devotion to your daughter is refreshing. She has brought him out of his shell. William and Georgiana are very shy and neither feel comfortable in large groups of people. William is the one to be in the corner trying to hide rather than in the middle of the group. It has always broke our hearts because he has so very much to share with the world. So what appears to be arrogance and disdain for others is in fact his fears and shyness. He does not like society, and if he had his way, he would stay at Pemberley always. That is where he can be himself. You will see when we go there. He is deeply respected by his servants and tenants. William is a very good Master, as he realizes that his wealth is due to the work of those very people who work for him. And he is not afraid to get his hands dirty. Gerald was the same way and taught his son to respect his heritage."

"A very wise choice. I cannot say I do the same. I have become very lax on my own estate when I should do more. After not having an heir and knowing the estate would be the property of my cousin, I did not care about working hard to improve. I allowed the estate to run itself because I did not wish to improve things only to have it benefit him."

"I cannot blame you there. It must have been a bitter pill to swallow. From what I have seen of Mr. Collins, I can understand your sentiments."

"His father was worse. He was a bitter man full of venom. I did not wish for him to benefit from my labor. Maybe I should take a lesson or two from William."

"I know that I wish my own sons to follow their cousin's good example. Now, as to the marriage settlement. I assume that your daughters have little more than their own goodness in a way of a dowry. If I remember you said something around one thousand pounds."

"They will have only one thousand pounds each as a dowry."

"Now they will have a dowry of thirty thousand each. We will need to discuss a 'distant cousin' who left them their inheritance. Also, I should have you know that my wife has already made a list of everything Elizabeth will need in her trousseau. And if you would allow it,

Elaine and I would be honored to take care of purchasing the trousseau as our wedding gift."

"I know that what Lizzy will need is going to be costly. My funds are limited and more towards marrying my daughters to ones of our society circle. But with her marrying into the first circle, there will be so many more items she will need. I will gladly accept your offer, but I do wish to purchase the dress Lizzy wears for the wedding. It will be the last dress I buy her before she leaves my home and name."

"That is a deal. And if my son's courtship turns into an attachment with Mary, we will make the same offer available."

"Henry, you and your wife are so highly appreciated. My daughters will be blessed for having new family as you. And may I say that you are definitely different from most people I have met of upper society."

"I tend to believe that it is due to their loveless marriages. When you treat your home and bed as a business transaction, it can only leave one bitter. So I feel I have bested them by loving my wife."

The men broke out in laughter.

Fitzwilliam and Mary walked to a beautiful clearing and decided to stop for a rest. "Miss Mary, I spoke to your father and asked for his permission to court you. He has given me permission. Does this meet with your liking?"

Mary blushed. She was so very shy around men, and had never found herself so much as attracted to a man before, let alone go on walks and enjoy long talks. "I would indeed welcome your courting me. I thank you Colonel."

"Please call me Richard."

"So, Richard, when do you return to your regiment?"

"I am on leave for now. But I tire of war and fighting. I would dearly love to leave that life and begin anew."

"What would you do?"

Richard smiled at Mary's question. "I would like a simpler life, with a good and loving woman at my side. A good home, maybe farm some. And chickens. My home has to have a pen full of chickens. I have always enjoyed laughing at the creatures."

Mary began to laugh. "They are indeed funny creatures. I have watched ours at Longbourn and find them humorous when the run about cackling."

"I long for a life with more enjoyment and less death. Cackling chickens running about sounds so much better than war. As the second son, my lot was laid in front of me. I made my choice for the regulars. Now, I have laid aside some money and would like very much to purchase a small piece of property and have a comfortable house. It would be no where near as extravagant as Rosing, and would pale horribly against Pemberley, but it would be comfortable for me."

"I feel living in such a large estate as this would be intimidating to me. What is Pemberley like?"

"Pemberley is quite large. Even more so than Rosings. But it has been furnished in a better way. Where you see so much ornamental and useless finery here, Pemberley is functional and practical. I enjoy staying there much more so than here. My Aunt Anne and Uncle Gerald, William and Georgiana's parents, felt that Pemberley was a grand estate, but it was first and utmost their home. Rosings is a house, Pemberley is a home. Does that make sense to you?"

"It does. I have seen the same even in our circle. Sir William Lucas, who is Mrs. Collins's father, has a more ornamental house than we do at Longbourn. My father has refused to allow my mother to purchase such frills, as he says he prefers to be comfortable in his home and the frills would make it more of an attraction for people to come visit like a museum."

"So very true. My parents are the same. We have a beautiful home but it is very frills free."

"Richard, I am truly enjoying the time we spend together. Does it sound awful to say I am grateful to Lizzy for her accident because it brought me here?"

A chuckle escaped Fitzwilliam's mouth. "If so, then we are both guilty for I was just thinking the same. I will be forever grateful to your sister for this."

"I have never so much as danced with a man or spoken more than a sentence or two with one at an assembly. And yet here I am speaking quite openly with you on many occasions. You are so very different than most men. I find great pleasure being around you."

Fitzwilliam raised Mary's hand to his lips and placed a light kiss on the back of it. "I have been able to have friendly conversations with others in my life, but never sharing my innermost feelings and wishes with anyone. I have not even discussed what I would like to do after years of military service with my parents. I know my mother would dearly love to have me safe and secure in a home, with a lovely wife and giving my mother grandchildren. My father fears my having to go to war again. I have come back year after year, but my luck will not hold out forever."

"I am glad that it has so far, for I cannot imagine a world without you in it. You are a great man Richard. Far better than I have ever met in my life. The men and boys I have met over the years are nothing in comparison to you."

"And you, Miss Mary, are quite remarkable. I am blessed to know you. Now, shall we begin to make our way back to the house?"

Mary nodded. "Richard, would you please call me Mary?" Fitzwilliam smiled and nodded in return.

Chapter 11

Lord Matlock ushered his son, Darcy, and Mr. Bennet into the study and shut the door. He then offered a glass of port to each man before he sat down. "I wish to discuss an important matter with you. And William, before you start worrying, Elizabeth is not in danger. No, I have enlightened Thomas here of an inheritance that has been in place for each of you young men and now I wish to discuss it with you. Gerald and I were both of a same mind when you boys were very young. We were both blessed with love in our marriages, and we wished for you to have the same. No marriages of convenience. No marriages made as business deals. They are not marriages but arrangements. You deserve true marriages. Knowing what most women of high society are like, Gerald and I preferred to keep your options open for finding someone to love no matter what her circumstances. So we decided to give you a gift."

"Each of us set up accounts which were kept private from you. Gerald set his up with me as controller in the case he was to die, and after his death I changed mine to Elaine in case I die. The accounts are this. They are dowries for your wives. The woman you choose to marry will have a dowry. Thomas and I will work out a distant relation for the inheritance to have come from for Elizabeth. Her dowry is thirty thousand. This will allow her to gain access to our circle of society without questions as to her motives being a fortune hunter, which we all know is not her reason for marrying you. But it will give her a chance to be accepted by our friends and once they get a chance to know her, they will love her for what she is to you William." Lord Matlock then turned to his own son.

"When you resign your commission from the regulars and decide to settle down, I have made provisions for a smaller estate on the other side of Pemberley for you. I purchased it many years ago in your name and the income from it has been building in an account since. There is over twenty thousand pounds in the account, and your wife's dowry will be the same as Elizabeth's. Together you will be worth fifty thousand pounds. The income from the estate is around two thousand per annum."

Both Darcy and Fitzwilliam were stunned and sat in silence. They both realized the extent of the generous gifts they had been given.

Mr. Bennet decided to add his thoughts. "I feel it best to claim a great aunt who had moved to the Americas to be one to give the inheritance. I think that if I claim her from my mother's side, no one would ever be the wiser. And, not to imply any attachment other than a courtship at this moment Fitzwilliam, but incase so we do not have to come up with a second long lost relative, my great aunt should be Mary Elizabeth. I will determine a last name on another day. Henry, how does that sound to you?"

"It sounds perfect. Then you can claim they had been named for this aunt. Men, how do you feel? Do you have any questions from either of us?"

Darcy smiled and thanked both Lord Matlock and Mr. Bennet. Fitzwilliam had a determined look on his face and finally came to a conclusion. "Mr. Bennet, I wish to resend my request from earlier. I know longer wish to court Miss Mary. I wish to ask for her hand in marriage."

This declaration did not come as a surprise to either of the fathers. Trying hard to control his laughter, Mr. Bennet looked at this man who had seen so much in his life. "Fitzwilliam, you are a very good man and I have come to respect you in the time I have known you.

Are you sure of your decision, as you have only known my daughter for such a short time."

"I have seen so much and done so much in my life, I do not wish to waste another moment searching the world for what I know I have in the woman in front of me. She is what I want for a wife. She is kind and loving, joyous to be with. She is wise beyond her years. We have enjoyed many talks in the time we have known each other. We share many of the same likes and interest. And she prefers a simpler life as do I. We discussed that very subject just a few hours ago. So, yes, Mr. Bennet, I do know that I love your middle daughter and wish to spend the rest of my life loving her."

Mr. Bennet smiled. "Well, I wish to discuss it with my daughter to be sure of her feelings but if she chooses you then I have no regrets in giving my permission to you marrying Mary. I would be proud to have you as another son. And as I told William, you may call me Father or Bennet. Or you men can call me Thomas as Henry here is now calling me." He shook the hands of both of the young men, then that of Lord Matlock. "It appears that this week will be written in our families histories as truly intertwined. Now, I will go and find Mary and discuss her opinion. Who knows, we may have another young man come to me while we are here and ask for yet another of my daughters for her hand. Maybe I should send for my younger two daughters, we could find someone for them and I could be done with all of this in just a few months." He laughed as he left the room.

"Well, Fitzwilliam, it appears that we will not only be cousins but we will be brothers as well. I have always thought of you as sort of a brother, so I am very pleased. I have also noticed a change in Mary, you have been very good for her."

After confirming Mary's desire to marry Fitzwilliam, Mr. Bennet went into the infirmary to see Elizabeth. "Papa, I am so glad to see you. I just woke a few moments ago."

"And how are you feeling? Is the pain subsiding any?"

"I feel as if I fell off a hill, which is true. My head is hurting some and my leg is constantly painful. But I feel quite fortunate."

"Well, since we have not had much of a chance to speak, I have some questions for you. The first is when did you determine that you were in love with William?"

"After he proposed, I was furious. You truly needed to have been there to hear how he had proposed. He told me how he wished to marry despite my obviously poor situation in life and how his family would look down upon the marriage. I made accusations against him as to his treatment of Wickham and of his separating Mr. Bingley from Jane. My pride was deeply wounded from his statements and what I felt was his bad behavior. He wrote a letter to me explaining his past with Wickham and of the evil things Wickham had done to his family."

"It was painful for William to open himself in such a way, for it also involved Wickham's attempt to elope with Georgiana. Wickham was willing to seduce a child for her dowry. The pain he inflicted upon both William and Georgiana was obvious. As to his reason to separate Mr. Bingley and Jane, there were two reasons. First he could not detect any partiality on Jane's part, and, if Jane was to marry William's best friend, he would constantly be forced to be near me."

"After I read the letter, I began to look at William in a different way. I realized that I had prejudices against him and had not given him a chance. As I was lost and scared, my thoughts continued to return to him, hoping he would come and find me and that I would have a chance to tell him that I realized that I had fallen in love with him and had feared to be honest with him. Papa, I just learned earlier today that William risked his own safety to come down on the ropes to bring me to safety. He did not send someone down, he could not imagine not coming down to me. He had to stand at the top of the hill while someone came with more ropes and a stretcher, standing there looking down at me and not knowing if I was still alive. He was the one who picked me up, placed me on the stretcher, and then brought me back up to safety. He was the one holding me as the doctor set my leg, holding me still as the pain was so severe and they did not wish me to thrash in pain and hurt myself worse."

Mr Bennet was truly moved by these revelations. "It was also William who made the painful decision for the ice bath. The doctor told us that either choice could end with your death. He recommended the ice, but there was a chance it would have killed you as well if the fever had continued. William stayed with you, along with Mary and Charlotte. Jane was too tender to stay in the room, so she sat with me. Mary told me how lovingly William was with you, his tears as he held on to hope of your survival. When the fever finally broke, it was William alone who picked you up from the ice and placed you on the table in the bathing chamber, then he removed from the room while the girls changed your clothing. He then returned you to this bed and was constantly by your side. William had not ventured further from this section of the house until tonight when

Lord Matlock and I spoke with him and Colonel Fitzwilliam in the study. I will allow William the right to speak to you of our talk later. But I want you to tell me, do you truly love William? Do not mistake gratitude or appreciation for love. Do you feel a complete and abiding love for him?"

With a smile, Elizabeth squeezed her father's hand. "I do love him Papa. I was foolish and now can see that I have been in love with him for some time, I just refused to admit to my feelings, as William had been unable to admit his."

"Very well. I am pleased. I will also tell you that you are not the only one of my daughters to be engaged."

"Mr. Bingley proposed to Jane?"

"Not yet. I am still waiting for his turn. No, Colonel Fitzwilliam and Mary are now engaged. And they are both quite pleased."

"Oh, my. Mama will be beside herself with flutters. So much has happened." Elizabeth wrinkled her face as a wave of pain hit her.

"Lizzy, are you well? Shall I fetch the doctor?"

"As much as I dislike the thought Papa, yes, please fetch him."

Mr. Bennet knew that her pain must be great if she was asking for the doctor to attend her. She had never liked anyone fussing over her, even when she was very ill.

Mr. Bennet knew the doctor had stepped outside for some fresh air. He went in search of the man. As soon as the doctor was found, he was brought in to see Elizabeth. Darcy saw the men as they entered the house and was immediately concerned and opened the door to the infirmary. He walked to Elizabeth's side and took hold of her hand. "What has happened Dearest?"

"Nothing to concern you over. The pain was intense and I admit that I wished the doctor to confirm that it was not worse than it was. I know that I have much recovering to do, I am just very impatient and dislike being forced to lie here for days. Do not panic, I am just being foolish."

"Foolish is not how I would describe you. But do not ask me to not panic. After seeing you through so much these few days, and learning of your love for me, I cannot help but to fear of anything which could take you away from me."

"I am going nowhere for now. I have no desire of being parted from you either. I simply need a dose of laudanum or something for the pain and allow myself the time needed to recover. I need to learn patience. Can you help me with that lesson?"

"I will try, though I am not well known for patience myself." Darcy smiled and placed a kiss on the palm of her hand. He turned to the doctor and Mr. Bennet. "Elizabeth is in pain. She wishes for something to ease it. What do you think Doctor?"

"Miss Elizabeth, I have been concerned with you not accepting anything for relief. I was going to speak with your father about that very issue this evening. If you do not take the medicine and allow yourself to relax while your body heals, it will take a much longer time before you are well."

"I am restless. I do not like lying still in bed for days. As my father can tell you, I have always been this way. But I am ready to learn to behave. I wish to recover as soon as I can so that I may enjoy my wedding. I will take your medicine and rest." Turning to Darcy she smiled. "I will do everything I can to behave myself. And I will learn to allow others to help me so I can give my body a chance to mend."

"Very good, Miss Elizabeth. Let me get the bottle and a spoon. I will be right back. I will also need to check all of your wounds to make sure you are healing properly. So gentlemen, if you would be so kind to step out and ask Miss Mary if she would come in to assist me."

The two men who loved Elizabeth more than anyone reluctantly stepped out of the room and sent a servant to find Mary. She came immediately, with Fitzwilliam in tow. The men stepped into Darcy's sitting room to wait. Time seemed to have stopped as the men waited. After an hour, Mary came back across to the men.

"The cuts and scrapes are healing and there is no sign of infection on any of them. The bruises are a very ugly color of greenish yellow, which the doctor says is a sign of healing. We checked her leg, and she is able to wiggle her toes, though it is painful to her. There is bruising on her leg, but it too has changed to a greenish yellow color. The doctor is certain she is on the mend, and he has been surprised that she has not allowed any medication until now. He knew that the pain had to be severe, and he was certain that if she would take the medication, it would allow her to rest so her body could do what it needed to. We have convinced her that if she wishes to leave for Pemberley next week, she has to take the pain medicine and get more sleep. And she promised to eat more when she is awake. Our threat is that she has to behave or she has to go to Longbourn rather than Pemberley."

This brought a round of laughter from the men. "Well, it appears that my middle daughter has finally stood her ground with her older sister. Bravo, Mary, well done. Richard, do you see the young lady you are marrying?"

Darcy stood and shook her hand. "My thanks to you Mary for your stubbornness with your sister. I will remember this threat if she does not behave."

"She is resting now, and the doctor feels she will sleep for at least a couple of hours. So, Richard, shall we go to the drawing room and continue to read?" Fitzwilliam stood and walked out of the room with his fiancé.

"I am so very surprised at the changes I am seeing in my daughters. Surprised and very pleased. Maybe we should bottle the water from here and sell it. As miraculous as it has been with my family, we could make a fortune." With a laugh, Mr. Bennet left the room and walked to the library.

Bingley and Jane had taken a walk in the park and had come to the small pond. There was a fallen tree lying on the ground and he led Jane to sit on it before taking a seat beside her.

"Jane, I wish to tell you why I disappeared so suddenly from Netherfield."

"There is no need Mr. Bingley. I understand that things change and you had to leave."

"Well, I just this week discovered the plot which was to remove me from the estate. Darcy finally told me of his role in the plot."

"Why would anyone wish to take you from Netherfield?"

"Let me tell you what I was told. When I left right after the ball, I went to London on business. What I did not know was that my sisters and Darcy had conspired against me and left to come to London to keep me there. I discovered them in London and was surprised as I was determined to return to Netherfield. They began speaking about missing London, disliking Hertfordshire, and such. When I expressed my wish to return to see you, the told me that you would not notice my absence as you were not smitten with me. They continued to tell me that you had no partiality towards me, and that they knew you to be interested in another. I foolishly listened and believed them. I only learned this week of your being in London for weeks after the holidays. I had no knowledge of it. Had I known, I would have paid a call on you. Darcy told me that my sisters received a call from you."

"Darcy told me that his reasons for aiding my sisters were two fold. He did not see any partiality on your part towards me and secondly Darcy was feeling attraction towards your sister even then and knew that if I were to continue my relationship and even further it with you, he would be thrown in the path of Miss

Elizabeth. He was not prepared to admit his feelings, and allowed your mother's and younger sisters' poor behavior as reasons against an attachment."

"I am shocked at all of this, though the most amazing is William's refusal to admit his attraction to Lizzy and using it to part us."

"Darcy told me this himself. It is one of the issues which caused her to first refuse his proposal. She was insistent of your constant affection towards me and of your heartbreak when I left. After finding Miss Elizabeth and taking her to Rosings for care, Darcy had the Colonel send an express to me requesting me to Rosings immediately. I was fearful of his dying so I jumped on my horse and made my way here. Upon my arrival, though I was slightly upset over his being fine, I grew concerned for your sister and in turn you for I know how dearly you love your sister. Darcy had told me the tale of separating me from you, finishing just moments before your arrival."

"What an incredible tale. And do you hold any animosity towards your friend? He did give us a second chance to be together and he admitted his behavior."

"I could not remain angry at Darcy, especially now that you have forgiven me and allowed me back into your life even before you knew the truth. Now that I have you back in my life, I do not wish to loose you again. Jane, I know in my heart that you are the one I wish to share my life with. Would you do me the honor of accepting my hand in marriage?"

A deep blush took over Jane's countinence. "Mr. Bingley, yes. Yes, a thousand times, yes. I wish to share my life with you.

Bingley embraced Jane and then jumped up shouting his joy. "Let us find your father. I wish to speak to him immediately to make this real. I know it may sound silly, but I fear anything coming between us now. Once I have his approval, the only thing left is for us to wed."

They went in search of Mr. Bennet and found him in the library. "Sir, I wish to request the honor of marrying your daughter Jane." Bingley blurted out quickly.

"Well, Mr. Bingley, I am shocked. I had no idea of your attraction to Jane." Mr. Bennet smiled at his eldest daughter. "I will have to consider this and give you my decision at a later time."

Bingley was deep red. "No Mr. Bennet, I have had members of my own family try to keep me from Jane and I am determined to marry her. As she is of age, I do not require your approval, but I am asking for it all the same. It is but a mere formality. If you refuse, I will take Jane to London immediately and be married as soon as we arrive. I am that determined."

"Mr. Bingley, I have been expecting your arrival to speak with me. I have been surprised only by your not coming sooner. I whole heartedly give my consent for your marriage to my eldest daughter.

There is no need to run off, as I have been teasing you only. I look forward to you being another one of my sons. As I have told William and Richard, you have the choice of calling me Father, Bennet or Thomas. You choose."

Jane came forward and embraced her father. "Thank you Papa. I as so very happy."

"As I am for you my dear. Now I have husbands for my eldest three daughters in one week. If there are men wishing to ask for Kitty and Lydia, I am quite at my leisure."

Chapter 12

Elizabeth woke feeling better. She was able to sit up slightly and she had a visit with Mary and Jane. The sisters were so very excited and each spoke of their love for the man they were each to wed. A knock on the door interrupted their cheerful glee. When Mary opened the door, it was to allow several servants to enter carrying trays of food and drink for the sisters to enjoy. One of the servants then spoke. "As Mr. Darcy has requested, Miss Elizabeth must eat to regain her strength. He said that if she resisted, that Miss Mary knew how to gain her cooperation." The servants then left.

This brought a round of giggles from the sisters. "Well, Lizzy, you had best begin so that I do not have to witness our sister's wrath descend." Jane was filled with joy.

"Lizzy knows that I have held my wrath for many years and it is now quite a fearsome thing to behold. So let us all partake of this fine feast William has sent us."

The sisters spent more than an hour conversing and enjoying the food. Finally, Mary took her newly found independence and insisted that it was time for Elizabeth to take another dose of medicine and rest some more. The newly discovered look of determination which resided in her expression told Elizabeth not to argue. The doctor came in and gave Elizabeth a dose of medicine as he checked on her condition. "Much better, Miss Elizabeth. This is what I told you would aid in your recovery."

Over the next few days, Elizabeth slept many hours. She was gaining strength each day and finally, she was able to sit up completely. Darcy decided to reward his betrothed by taking her to the drawing room after dinner that evening. Everyone was so pleased to see her looking so much better and they each came forward to embrace her. Georgiana had been keeping Anne company as Anne was learning her new position from Lady Matlock, and was now so pleased to see her soon to be sister recovering. "May I play a song for you, Miss Elizabeth?"

"Miss Darcy, as I am soon to be married to William, you should call me Elizabeth. Would you approve if I called you Georgiana?"

"Oh, yes, Elizabeth. I would love for you to call me Georgiana. I am so thrilled to have you become my sister. What is your favorite song? I will play it on the pianoforte."

This was the most animated Darcy had seen his sister since Ramsgate. Elizabeth smiled at how Georgiana was adapting. "Surprise me Georgiana. I wish to hear whatever you choose to play."

After three songs, Elizabeth was tiring. Darcy carried her back to the infirmary for the doctor to do his usual check on her wellness and administer another dose of medicine. "Do you feel you will be able to travel to Pemberley in a few more days? I have already sent for our personal surgeon to come from London to travel with us to Pemberley, and then the surgeon from Lambton will meet us at

Pemberley when we arrive. I wish for only the best of care for you."

"I think that if we do not rush the ride, I should do fine. I will take my medicine and most likely sleep most of the trip."

"I have ordered a special carriage to come from London with the surgeon. It will allow you to sleep in comfort. Doctor Jameson and I will be riding with you. It has extra padding and comforts as well as a stretcher inside for your to lay on."

"My goodness William. I would feel like royalty to be transported in such a manner. It is not necessary. I will be fine in one of your good carriages."

"No, I wish for you to not have a set back from our travel. This will allow you the comfort as well. The trip will be over a two day period. I could not bear to have you sitting up and in pain for so long a ride."

"Only because you would be more at ease will I accept such luxury. My thanks, beloved. You think of everything."

"We received a letter from my god father. The Arch Bishop of Derby is pleased to learn of my plans to wed such a wonderful woman and insists on the honor of presiding over the vows, and doing so before he leaves on his trip of the continent. He leaves for the continent on April eighteenth. He would like a few days between the wedding and his departure, so he begs to have the wedding the week before if possible.

In speaking with your father and my uncle, we have decided on April eleventh for the nuptials, if that would please you."

"I would love for that day to be our wedding day. For in case my father did not already inform you, it is also my birthday. It would be fitting for the day I come of age to also be my wedding day."

A smile showed Darcy's deep dimples. "I was not aware of the fact, but now can think of nothing better for our wedding date. I love you, Elizabeth. I love you so very dearly."

Mary and Fitzwilliam were preparing for her to leave with her family while he stayed temporarily at Rosings with his as they were aiding Anne with her taking over the estate. They would be a week apart, and the new couple was already feeling the pangs of separation. "I plan to go to London on my way north to Pemberley. I will be resigning my commission before I come to you at my cousin's estate. I may be a day behind my parents' arrival."

"But after that, I will no longer fear loosing you to some war. It will be difficult, but I will be pleased to reunite with you."

"We have not discussed a wedding date. When would you prefer to wed? Do you wish to have an extended engagement or would you prefer to follow in Elizabeth and William's method? I will be moving into my new estate the week prior to their wedding."

"I wish we could just join Lizzy and William, and move on to our life together."

"I could speak with Darcy and ask for his consent. The arch bishop is my father's cousin. I am sure he would approve of presiding over our wedding as well."

"Do you truly believe they would approve of our decision? What of your parents? Will they be pleased with our choice?"

"Let us ask and see."

The couple went in search of Darcy and Fitzwilliam's parents. Once they were together, Fitzwilliam was nervous. "We wish to ask a favor of you Darcy. We would like to know if we could share your wedding day. Mary and I do not wish to wait and we do not desire a large wedding. We prefer a quiet wedding as you and Elizabeth have chosen."

Lady Matlock was thrilled, pulling Mary into an embrace. "I will have a daughter so soon. I am so very pleased. I tire of all the men in my family and look forward to having a female cohort."

"Cousin, Mary, I will speak with Elizabeth about this, but I feel safe in saying that we would be honored to be married side by side with you."

"Oh, my, not only do we have to prepare Elizabeth's trousseau, but now we will have to hurry to prepare yours. No fear. Richard, you were stopping in London were you not, on your way to Pemberley? Will you take a letter to Mrs. Whitaker's shop? I will tell her what we need, and have her bring some of her staff and items we need to Pemberley. I know William has arranged for the Lambton modiste for Elizabeth, so between the two staffs, we should be able to pull this off." Lady Matlock went to find some stationary and begin her list of demands from Mrs. Whitaker's shop. There would not be as great a demand on formalities for Mary as there were for Elizabeth, as Elizabeth is becoming Mrs. Darcy. Elizabeth will be watched closer than Mary, for Richard had never been the marked interest of matchmakers as his cousin had been since his majority. But there would still be many items to address.

Mary and Fitzwilliam went to find Mr. Bennet and announce their plans. He was pleased to hear the news and made the same insistence of paying for the wedding dress for his daughter. He was told Lady Matlock's plans to request her personal modiste to come from London and the preparations she was making for the trousseau. Mr. Bennet chuckled as he thought of his wife and how she would be disappointed by not having control over her daughters' weddings. He knew he now had to write to his wife and announce the plans which were now coming together. It would be a long letter and she would be in great need of her smelling salt when she read it.

After dinner that night, Elizabeth again graced the drawing room with her presence. The room was filled with so much joyous talk about the double wedding and all of the plans which were needed to be done before hand. Suddenly, Jane stood up in front of everyone and made an announcement. "Charles and I wish also to marry on April eleventh. May we make the wedding a triple service? I have always thought of having a big wedding, but the more I think of it, the more I feel my sisters are choosing the correct way."

Elizabeth and Mary both laughed as the men came to clap Bingley on his shoulders. Mr. Bennet stood up and looked at his daughters. "I feel the need to send for more smelling salts to be sent to Longbourn when my next letter arrives for your mother. I feel we will be able to hear her all the way here when she begins her effusions. Men, feel grateful you are so far from my wife, as your eardrums will be saved. I know that I am pleased with my location as well."

"We are all enjoying our hearing ability due to being so far from Mama. Perhaps you should warn the apothecary before Mama receives your letter so that he would be able to supply her with treatment for her nerves." Elizabeth laughed at her teasing of her mother's deficiencies. The entire room was filled with laughter. "Well, Papa, the only question is going to be how to bring all three of your daughters up the aisle at the same time."

"Lizzy, that will be quite simple as you will be in a wheeled chair, and we can have one of your sisters on each side of the chair. So your not being able to actually walk up the aisle will be a benefit rather than a detriment."

"It is my pleasure to be of such an aid to the services. Now, shall we allow Mama to plan Jane's trousseau? Then she will not feel quite so left out from all the plans?"

Jane looked somewhat concerned at this thought, but she decided that with the help of all of her family around her, she would be able to control her mother's enthusiasm.

Chapter 13

Screams of joy were heard from Longbourn as she read an express letter she received from her husband. Her first three daughters were all to be married on the same day, three very advantageous marriages, and the weddings would be presided over by an Arch Bishop at Pemberley's chapel. As much as she would prefer to have the weddings from Longbourn so that she could show the neighborhood how very well her daughters were marrying, to have the marriage vows solemnized by an Arch Bishop was very prestigious. She read how Mr. Darcy had already commissioned a modiste to prepare Elizabeth's trousseau, and Lady Matlock was having her personal modiste to prepare Mary's. This left Jane's trousseau for Mrs. Bennet to help prepare. She was told that the staff from Lady Matlock's modiste would also assist Mrs. Bennet, as the modiste would bring more staff to handle both of the brides' needs.

The men had requested special licenses which the Arch Bishop had arranged for.

This was another feather in Mrs. Bennet's bonnet to crow over. She quickly wrote to her sister Gardiner in London and began her list of what would be needed for her eldest daughter's marriage. Plans were made for the remaining Bennet sisters and their mother to travel to Pemberley on March twentieth. Though time would be limited, Mrs. Bennet had been assured that the staff of Pemberley would be able to assist with the demands of all the arrangements. Dresses would also have to be made for Lydia and Kitty, as well as something new for Mrs. Bennet herself.

"Oh, how clever of Lizzy to attract Mr. Darcy, as she has placed her sisters in the way of other wealthy men. Now we will have to have her find husbands for you girls." Mrs. Bennet squealed at her youngest daughters as they went to the Meryton dressmaker's shop. "I knew Lizzy was quite clever and look at what she has done. Her accident was quite effective in sealing her attachment with Mr. Darcy."

As they arrived in Meryton, the girls were approached by two of their favorite officers from the militia. Lt. Denny and Lt. Wickham were pleased to see the young ladies and decided to escort them the rest of the way to the shop.

"So, what are you planning to order at the shop? A new dress for a ball?" Wickham asked Lydia. "Is there an assembly planned for soon? I have so desired to dance with you again."

"We are ordering dresses for a triple wedding. Our sisters are marrying next month."

"Miss Bennet, Miss Elizabeth and Miss Mary are all marrying on the same day? How amazing. And who are they marrying?"

"Jane is marrying Mr. Bingley, Elizabeth to Mr. Darcy, and Mary to Colonel Fitzwilliam, Mr. Darcy's cousin."

"My, this is shocking. How did this all come about? Mr. Bingley and Mr. Darcy left Hertfordshire quite some time ago. How did Mary come to meet Colonel Fitzwilliam?" Wickham was filled with questions of his childhood friend, the friend whom he found great pleasure in torturing. He would have to learn all he could about this turn of events and decide how best to give his 'old friend' a wedding gift he would not soon forget.

"Have you not heard about Elizabeth's accident?"

"Remember, Miss Lydia, I was recently sent to Brighton with papers to deliver for Colonel Forrester. I have only just returned. You say Miss Elizabeth had an accident?"

"Oh, yes. Lizzy was visiting our cousin, Mr. Collins, and his wife Charlotte, at their home at Hunsford. This is the parsonage attached to Rosings Park, the home of Mr. Darcy and Colonel Fitzwilliam's aunt, Lady Catherine. Mr. Darcy and the Colonel were visiting their aunt when Lizzy was caught outside in a severe and sudden storm. She lost her way and fell off a hill. They were delayed by the storm's severity to begin the search. It was over a full day before they were able to locate Lizzy and she was not only badly injured but also developed a deadly high fever. She has recovered from this, but in the mean time, Mr. Bingley, my father and sisters all arrived at Rosings. I do not know any further details, with the exception that they will all be travelling to Pemberley next week and the grand wedding will be on April eleventh. They have all received special licenses and are to be married by an Arch Bishop. It is all so very romantic. We leave on the twentieth of this month for Pemberley as well."

"I hope you find the estate as enjoyable as I always did."

"I forgot, you grew up there. What is it like?"

"It is quite large, and has a beautiful park. I enjoyed many hours there. I wish to one day be allowed to return to my childhood haunts, but, so far, Mr. Darcy has continued to dislike me for my being his father's favorite. Maybe your sister will be able to convince him to overlook his jealousy and allow my entrance to Pemberley again."

"I can only hope, for I would like you to be able to enjoy visiting there."

"Well, here we are at the shop. Miss Lydia, it has been a pleasure speaking with you today. It has been very enlightening. I hope to see you soon."

"Good day Mr. Wickham. Thank you for walking us here."

Wickham was dismayed. Darcy falling in love with a nobody like Elizabeth Bennet. He thought for years that Darcy would give in to his aunt and marry his sickly cousin Anne. And Fitzwilliam? He was also marrying, and for it to be the sermonizing Mary Bennet. Wickham was surprised that the Colonel would leave the regulars for a marriage, as he was a second son. What was the attraction to Mary who did not have a dowry which was necessary for Fitzwilliam to marry? The marriage of Bingley and Jane Bennet was not surprising, it was expected last fall. And they were all at Rosings. Lady Catherine must have been sedated to allow all of this to bloom in her home.

Wickham had to determine a way to ruin Darcy's happiness, as Darcy had ruined Wickham's chances to secure Georgiana's dowry. How dare Darcy find love and joy when he stole Wickham's chance at having a beautiful and naïve young wife and thirty thousand pounds to do what he wished with. The thought of ruining Georgiana had been a delicious form of revenge, now Wickham would have to find another way which would be equally rewarding.

The medical carriage and Doctor Jameson arrived and preparations were made for the journey to begin from Rosings to Pemberley. Anne had declared herself in control of her estate so as to send her relatives on to prepare for the weddings. She would travel to Pemberley a few days before the service, coming with the Collins family. Lady Catherine declined to travel and would be kept company by Anne's companion Mrs. Jenkinson.

Mr. Bennet would travel in his carriage with Jane and Bingley. Darcy's carriage would transport Fitzwilliam, Mary, Georgiana and Georgiana's companion, Mrs. Annesley. Lord and Lady Matlock would travel alone. Servants would be following in a separate carriage.

Doctor Jameson gave Elizabeth a heavy dose of medication so she would sleep as they moved her and settled into the medical carriage. He knew how painful it would be and wished for Elizabeth not to have to endure it. It would also keep Darcy calm not to have to witness his betrothed's pain. Having been Darcy's doctor for many years, he knew that

Darcy took his responsibility to ones he loved very deeply. When Georgiana was twelve, she developed a case of influenza. Darcy was beside her day and night, ordering anything needed to save his sister and guarantee her comfort. Doctor Jameson could only imagine what the past week had been for the Hunsford surgeon to endure, especially when it was obvious how deeply Darcy loved his fiancé.

Elizabeth was placed on the stretcher in the carriage, a cover pulled over her and tucked in around her. She was peacefully sleeping, her hair draped across the pillow below her head. Darcy took the seat near her head, and the doctor took the seat near her feet. They each brought with them items to care for Elizabeth on the journey. Darcy brought books to read to her, as well as food and drink for when she was awake. Doctor

Jameson brought medications which would aid her sleep and take away her pain. He also had extra bandaging incase any of her wounds opened on the trip.

The trip was taken at a moderate rate, making stops as needed along the way to care for Elizabeth's needs as well as the needs of all the other travelers.

They were near Pemberley when Elizabeth woke. "Look out the window dearest. This is our home." Elizabeth was able to lift her head enough to look outside and gasped as she took in her new home. "William, it is beautiful. And so big. How am I ever to be able to find my way around such a large house, let alone be Mistress of it?"

"Elizabeth, I have run the estate for five years without a wife. I have an excellent staff. As your health improves, you can learn from Mrs. Reynolds which responsibilities you wish to take over. You are not expected to take over all the duties nor are you expected to take on any duties immediately. First and most important is your healing. Second is our wedding. After that, we will discuss Pemberley." He placed a kiss on his beloved Elizabeth's forehead.

Doctor Jameson pulled out his medical bag to prepare another dose of medicine for his patient. "Please, William, I do not wish the first time I enter our home to be on a stretcher and unconscious. Can we wait until we are inside before I take another dose of medicine?"

"Miss Elizabeth, it will be quite painful for us to remove you from the carriage and carry you inside the house, not to mention getting you settled into the infirmary here. Are you sure you can bear such pain? With your leg being bumped and the cuts and bruises, the pain may be excruciating? As much as they have healed, it would not take a lot of jostling around to cause them to trouble you again. Especially the wound on your head. I do not wish to see it reopen and become infected."

"Please dearest, take the medicine. The staff will not be assembling as I have already informed Mrs. Reynolds as to your condition and how you were being transported. We will have a formal introduction to the staff in a week, once you have had a chance to rest. Please do not make me bare seeing you in such pain when I know it can be prevented."

Elizabeth looked into the eyes of this very strong man who was begging for her to be out of pain. For his sake, she decided to do as he bid and she swallowed her dose of medicine. As the carriage stopped in front of the stairs leading to the front entrance, Elizabeth's eyes were fluttering closed. She vaguely remembered later seeing the front of her new home before drifting off. Darcy stepped out of the medical carriage and motioned for the footmen to come forward.

Two men were to carry the foot of the stretcher, and two were to carry the head. Doctor Woodland was at the front door watching the men carrying his new patient from the carriage. She was an attractive young lady, even with her injuries and being unconscious. Doctor

Woodland had delivered both Darcy and Georgiana and was quite accustomed with the family. He watched Darcy's expression as he ordered his staff as to how Elizabeth was to be handled, constantly telling them to be careful. Doctor Jameson followed closely behind Darcy, and the look on his face made it clear that he felt Darcy should have been sedated as well. This brought a smile to Doctor Woodland's face. Obviously Darcy was deeply in love.

Elizabeth was taken into the infirmary and before placed into the bed, Mrs. Reynolds had four maids prepared to bathe the soon to be Mistress. After the bath, she was dressed in a night shift and robe before being placed on the bed and covered with several coverlets. Doctor Woodland had discussed all of Elizabeth's injuries and the fever with Jameson. The two doctors inspected her injuries to confirm they were still healing, and to re-bandage her head wound and broken leg. Just as they were finishing the examination, Elizabeth began to awaken.

"Welcome to your new home, Miss Elizabeth. I am Doctor Woodland, and I have just finished discussing all of your health with Doctor Jameson. Now, how are you feeling? You have been through much today, are you ready for something to eat before you have some more medicine?"

"Doctor Woodland? We are at Pemberley are we not? I am a little foggy at the moment."

Doctor Jameson stepped forward. "We gave you a slightly stronger dose of medicine this last time. We knew that not only would it be painful for you to be brought in, but before you were placed in the bed, we decided to bathe you and redress your wounds. A very painful procedure, and if we had not heavily sedated you, we would have had to do so for your betrothed. As it was, Doctor Woodland and I were tempted to slip something to Mr. Darcy when he was unaware."

Elizabeth gave a weak laugh. "I am sure the staff wished that you had done just that. He can be quite the mother hen, when he wishes."

"How very correct you are. Fortunately I have known Mr. Darcy all of his life and know when to ignore his behavior. I was the doctor who brought him into the world, so I feel safe in saying I know him extremely well. I have seen him through his best times and, definitely, through his worst times." Doctor Woodland was very friendly and pleasant. "Now, are you going to be a good patient and do as you are told or are you going to be someone we need to restrain to the bed to gain your cooperation?"

Doctor Jameson laughed at his counterpart. "From what I understand, her younger sister, Mary, who was in one of the other carriages, is very good at threats to keep her sister in line. Though, I feel that we can also find her husband to be quite useful in achieving the necessary goal."

"Gentlemen, I have no intention to be anything other than the perfect patient for I wish to be well and able to marry my beloved William on the eleventh. I will do

what is necessary to achieve this goal."
Elizabeth stated softly.

"Now, if you would send my dear William in, I will allow him to witness my behaving and eating before I sleep some more." She had a very sweet smile on her face as she made it quite clear she would placate everyone so she could mend as quickly as possible.

Darcy entered the infirmary and walked over to the side of the bed. Taking Elizabeth's hand, he smiled at her. "How do you feel, dearest?"

"I have had a bath and dressed in clean clothes, placed here in this comfortable bed, and had my injuries redressed and now wish to enjoy some nourishment with you before being a good girl and taking my medicine and sleeping more. Would you please join me in partaking of my first meal in our home?"

"I will join you for our first meal together at Pemberley and join you everyday for the rest of our lives." Darcy pulled on the cord to request a servant to bring trays to them. Before he could finish his request, Mrs. Reynolds came in with several servants carrying trays.

"Miss Elizabeth, it is a pleasure to meet you. I am Mrs. Reynolds, and if there is anything you require, you need only ask. We have two nurses who will take turns staying with you, especially through the night. The doctor's room is across the hall and a door down. I have also prepared the room across the hall for you Master William, as I knew you would be hard pressed to go upstairs at any time soon. We have escorted all of the guests to the rooms they will occupy while they are here, most are cleaning up and resting from the trip. We will have dinner ready for them in an hour's time. I knew you would wish to eat privately and together, and the doctor will be giving Miss Elizabeth some medicine after eating to keep her pain level down as well as allow her to sleep."

"As I told you dearest, Mrs. Reynolds has been like a grandmother to me and she knows me so very well."

"Also, we can discuss tomorrow the other plans which you wrote me of. I have contacted the modiste, as well as sent out inquiries for a lady's maid for Miss Elizabeth. We will be expecting the arrival of your other guests as they arrive. Are there any others we should be made aware of coming? Are Mr. Bingley's sisters coming?"

"Mrs. Hurst and her husband are at his parents' estate right now and they will not be able to come. Hurst's father has become ill. Miss Bingley has decided to stay in London, as her brother is quite angered at her and Mrs. Hurst for their interference in his affairs. I think that the only guests we are still expecting are Elizabeth's mother and younger two sisters, Colonel Fitzwilliam, and Lady Anne de Bourgh." The last name made Mrs. Reynold's eyebrow rise. A slight nod from Darcy was all that was needed to confirm that Anne had taken over as Mistress of Rosings. "Anne will be arriving with a Mr. and Mrs. Collins who are Elizabeth's cousin and her dear friend. Am I forgetting anyone, dear?"

"My Aunt and Uncle Gardiner with their four children. I do not think there are any other family members from our side of the family."

"I do believe that is all of our expected guests. I know how few rooms we have, will we need to place cots in the ballroom for the guests?"

Mrs. Reynolds noted the levity of her master, something she had not seen in him in many years. "It will be tight sir, but I do believe we will be able to manage. So far we do not have to place anyone in the servants' house." She smiled and made to leave the room.

"Mrs. Reynolds, I wish to thank you for all of your hard work. I know we have brought so much work on you and the staff. Please know how grateful we are. And thank your staff for us. I know the next few weeks will be a whirlwind, so I do not wish to forget to show my appreciation."

"All the thanks we need is seeing Master William and Miss Georgiana happy. I can already see the love you have for Master William, as well as he has for you. I will leave you to your meal and we will talk at a later time. If you need anything, just pull the cord."

After they ate, Elizabeth allowed Doctor Woodland to give her medicine and drifted off to sleep. Darcy went across the hall to the room which had been prepared for him. He laid his head on the pillow and drifted off to pleasant dreams. His future was coming together and he was happier than he had ever known in his life.

The rest of the week was frantic for most of the occupants of Pemberley. The upcoming triple wedding had so many plans to carry out, so many details to confirm with each couple.

Mrs. Bennet and her daughters arrived and the atmosphere in the house became tense. Because she was not in charge of planning the wedding, she placed all of her attention towards Jane's needs for the wedding. Mrs. Bennet made lists of what she felt was necessary for her first born's trousseau, especially as Jane was marrying so well. She, also, questioned all of her daughters as to why they would keep to such small weddings as they were all marrying such important men. Mrs. Bennet felt it would be better to have the weddings be a social event of the season, with everyone who was invited speaking of it for ages. All of her daughters informed Mrs. Bennet of their desires for the wedding, and how they only wished for their new lives to begin. The frills were not important to them. The only part that they cared about was their chosen husband be waiting for them at the alter. Nothing else mattered to each of the young ladies.

Fitzwilliam arrived at Pemberley with the news that he was now a country gentleman, and his red coat was forever more to be placed in storage. He began to prepare his new home at Newbury Hall for his new life, including preparations for bringing his bride to their estate. As it had been many years since anyone had resided in the house on the estate, there was much to prepare. Fitzwilliam would come to Pemberley daily, telling Mary of his accomplishments of the day and asking for her advice on other changes which needed addressing. They spent many hours discussing their new home and their likes. Jane and Bingley went with Fitzwilliam and Mary to Newbury to view it, and all were impressed. The estate was close to the size of Longbourn, and the house was sound. The furnishings were older, though still quite sturdy and showed very little wear. It was functional, not decorated ornately. This was a preference of both Fitzwilliam and Mary.

Chapter 14

Jane and Bingley began to discuss their future. Bingley knew that living at Netherfield would bring Mrs. Bennet to their home on a regular basis. As dearly as Bingley had come to appreciate Mr. Bennet, Mrs. Bennet left a desire to be far away. Also, Lydia and Kitty would be in constant demands for their own comfort. No, it would be best to let go of Netherfield after the lease ran out. They would speak with Darcy about any properties in Derbyshire which might be available.

Each day, Elizabeth grew stronger. Darcy kept a close watch over her and if he felt she was overwhelmed, he would set his foot down. The modiste came and took measurements, patterns were chosen, and preferences were noted. Darcy told the seamstress that no expense was to be spared in making his wife's trousseau. And he would pay a bonus for having half of the order delivered before the wedding.

Lady Matlock's modiste arrived with eight of her staff, prepared to design Mary's trousseau and assist in Jane's. A staggering amount of fabrics, lace and ribbons would be necessary. The ballroom was turned into a dressmaker's shop for the convenience of the modistes and their staff, giving them easier access to the young ladies for fittings and consultations. This was Mrs. Bennet's area of excitement, the only area which she was allowed any say.

Mrs. Whitaker also brought with her a cobbler and a furrier so footwear and winter coats could be ordered. She had also brought several young men she used to relay requests to and from London. Lady Matlock knew that there were items such as hair accessories, and stationary, perfumes, hairbrushes, and much more that would need to be purchased, especially for Mary, as Richard would have no idea of what his bride would need. Darcy had lived with Georgiana long enough to know some of the items needed, and Mrs. Bennet would see to Jane's necessities.

Jane chose for her wedding dress a silk of pure white. It was to have beautiful embroidery on the bodice, and would have a bonnet to match. Mary chose a silk of the palest green, as it would bring out the color of her eyes. For Elizabeth, her dress would be of a beautiful pale yellow silk, the dress she had dreamed of owning.

Each of the grooms had a particular piece of jewelry to present to their intended. Bingley had his mother's sapphire and pearl necklace for Jane.

Darcy had the jewelry of his ancestors, but chose a diamond choker for his bride to wear at their wedding. Fitzwilliam was surprised by his mother who gave him a necklace of emeralds which had been in her family for generations. She wished for him to have some pieces of his family's history, as the other men and his brother would have, to give the women they loved.

Elizabeth was grateful for the use of the wheeled chair, for it gave her a bit more independence than she would have had if she were to depend on someone to carry her. Though having the strong arms of her handsome intended firmly holding her close to him sent shivers of delight coursing through her.

Mrs. Reynolds was in charge of the wedding breakfast, though she was given much advice from the mother of the brides. Georgiana took charge of the decorations for the chapel and music for the service.

The days went by quickly as the preparations were made. There was little time for the grooms to be alone with their ladies, which was agonizing for both sides. The final week before the wedding brought the final guests to arrive. Little else was discussed each day. Lord Matlock and Mr. Bennet decided to take the young men for some sport to relieve their stress. Lady Matlock decided to take Mrs. Bennet into Lambton to give the young ladies a much needed afternoon of peace.

The morning of the weddings was chaotic. Preparing one bride for her walk to her husband was enough work, but when there were three brides, the preparations were endless.

The men were taken to the chapel, to keep them from seeing their brides. Mrs. Bennet flitted from one of her daughters to the next, checking their hair and dress and jewels to ensure they were perfect. Elizabeth would wear a piece of ivory lace on her head instead of a wedding bonnet. Mary decided on a bonnet covered in green lace.

When the time finally arrived, Mr. Bennet moved Elizabeth's wheeled chair in between his other two daughters. Jane and Mary each placed a hand on top of their father's as his hands were on the back of the wheeled chair. The door to the chapel opened, and Mr. Bennet walked his three eldest daughters up the aisle to their futures.

The wedding was beautiful, and Mr. Bennet had to wipe tears from his eyes several times. He watched, as each of his daughters were pronounced wives, and the love in the eyes of their husbands was quite obvious. The wedding breakfast was wonderfully conducted, with course after course of delicious food. Mrs. Bennet cooed over how important her new sons were.

Bingley and Jane left for London for a week in their townhouse. Caroline Bingley had left it after being sent a message of her brother and his wife coming. Fitzwilliam and Mary decided to honeymoon at their new home. The last to leave were the Darcys. It was decided that they would go to a cottage the Fitzwilliam family owned which was isolated and had been the wedding night location for many generations. Darcy was at first concerned with such a plan, though he was reassured by Doctor Woodland of Elizabeth being well recovered with the exception of her broken leg. To give her husband an added sense of relief, Doctor Woodland wrapped Elizabeth's splint as sturdy as possible.

The Bennets, and Lord and Lady Matlock would stay at Pemberley for the week while Darcy and Elizabeth would be at the cottage. Georgiana was pleased to have her aunt and uncle to assist her in hosting the Bennets, as she was not yet comfortable in large groups.

Upon arriving at the cottage, Darcy carried his bride inside. For a cottage, the building was quite large. This brought a laugh from Elizabeth as she realized just what her husband considered small in housing. There was a cook, a housekeeper, a footman, and the valet and personal maid of the Darcys. There was a sitting room, a dining room, a study, the kitchen, four bedchambers, dressing rooms, and water closets. The cottage had been used for many different purposes, but the most pleasant was for the Fitzwilliam family members to begin their marriages.

Darcy carried his wife to the master suite, taking her into her dressing room where her maid, Rebecca, was preparing to tend to her Mistress. "I will return for you in an hour, if that is agreeable with you." Elizabeth smiled and nodded. Darcy then walked to his own dressing room to have Rogers assist him.

An hour later, there was a knock on the dressing room door. Rebecca opened the door and then excused herself from the suite. She and Rogers would be downstairs in the servants' quarters until they were called for. Darcy took a quick breath as he took in the beautiful sight in front of him. Elizabeth wore a silk nightdress, deep burgundy in color, with her hair down around her shoulders. She wore a provocative smile on her face and a twinkle in her eyes. He took her into his arms and carried her into the bedchamber. He laid her on top of the bed, reaching his hand to her face, caressing her cheek. "Elizabeth, you are so very beautiful. I love you."

"And I love you William. I am pleased to see your neck and chest. Your shirts and cravats hide these from view. You are quite handsome, my William."

Darcy leaned forward and caressed her lips lightly with his. Slowly at first, his hunger for her built into a frenzy. His tongue begged entrance into her and her lips parted to give him way. He tasted her mouth, exploring every part as his appetite grew. His lips then began to move over her, to her jaw, down her neck where he lightly nibbled. Elizabeth began a soft moan as her husband found sensitive parts of her body. Darcy untied the ribbons of the night dress and lowered the dress to expose her breasts. His hand began to discover the wonders of her breasts, caressing soft circles around the soft mounds. He then moved to take her breast into his mouth, suckling her as she writhed beneath him. Her fingers were tangled in his hair, holding his head to her as he brought her pleasure.

Darcy then returned his attention to her mouth as she ran her fingers over his body. The sensation was exquisite to him. "Lizzy, may I remove the night dress? I wish to see all of you." She nodded her answer and he saw her passion building in her expression. Darcy lifted himself to the side of his bride, pulling her night dress completely off of her and tossing it on the floor. "So very beautiful, dearest. I have dreamed of you so many times. But never in my wildest dreams did I ever come close to your true beauty." His mouth returned to claim hers, finding an insatiable thirst for her taste.

Soon, Elizabeth's hands were pulling the remaining buttons of her husband's shirt open and moved inside the shirt over his body. Finally, so thrilled with his wife's touch, Darcy ripped his shirt off his body and threw it somewhere on the floor. Elizabeth's hands glided down to his breeches, and as her slight touch sent waves of ecstasy through him, he let out a deep moan. Elizabeth was concerned she had harmed him and pulled her hand away. "No, my love. Please." Darcy pulled her hand back to his amorous arousal, showing her how to please him. Elizabeth unbuttoned the fall of his breeches, allowing his arousal the freedom it desired. Darcy slid his hand between Elizabeth's thighs, encouraging them to part to give entrance to the pearl of her womanhood. He caressed gently upwards, until his fingers found their way to her gentle folds. Slowly, he entered his fingers into portal, as Elizabeth arched towards his touch. The wetness of her body told him she was ready for him.

Darcy stood up and quickly removed his final piece of clothing. He then regained his position on top of Elizabeth as he guided his manhood to claim her body. Slowly he entered her, watching her closely as to not cause her pain. When he came to her final barrier, he looked into her eyes. "There may be some pain, dearest. Are you sure you are ready?"

"William, make me yours. I love you." No further words were needed. Darcy thrust inside her, and then slowly building a rhythm as he allowed her lush, tight womanhood to caress his arousal. With each delicious thrust, Darcy found his home in the woman he loved. Over and over, as his wife writhed from pleasure, Darcy thrust further and further inside her. She found her peak just a moment before he found his. His release brought such joy to him. He collapsed in euphoric bliss. When he was finally able to think again, he looked in his wife's eyes. "Are you well, my love?"

Elizabeth smiled a very satisfied grin. "So very well. Oh, my dearest, I have never been better." She kissed his lips and embraced him.

Darcy held her tightly in his arms. "I never knew how wonderful loving you could be. As I dreamed of this moment, I knew we would be happy and our love would be special. But the feelings I have just experienced were so very heavenly. Words cannot express how you have made me feel."

"Now I am yours. I am completely yours forever more."

"Elizabeth, you have held every part of me since the moment I first saw you. Now I will always know what heaven is, for I have found it in your arms." Darcy rested his head against the back of hers, his warm breath tickling her ear. As they lay spooned together, his hands took possession of her breasts. Gently he continued to caress her breasts, as she reveled from the pleasure.

Soon, they were both eagerly desiring the other. This time was different, very fevered in their passion, Darcy's thrusts were strong and fast. The bed shook with each powerful thrust, each one entering further and further inside his beloved. She clung to him, whispering words of love as she begged for him to complete her. They both found bliss at the same moment. As his seed filled her, he sank onto his bride, kissing her neck and face.

Darcy and Elizabeth fell asleep in each others arms. Hours later, Darcy woke with a feeling of wholeness. As he looked down at the sleeping beauty in his arms, he knew that his life was perfect.

Elizabeth started to wake, with an impertinent smile gracing her lips. "Well, Mrs. Darcy, what could inspire such a look?"

"I was just thinking of how generous and giving my handsome husband is. I cannot remember what life was before I loved him."

"He is not near as generous as his wife though. The bounty of pleasure she has given makes her a true angel."

"My dear, angelic is the furthest thing from my thoughts at the moment, sir. My thoughts are more of a wanton nature."

"I am so very pleased to hear this, as they will match your husband's thoughts as well. But before we investigate these thoughts further, I insist we enjoy some of the splendid food which has been left for us. I will not have you become weak from starvation while I ravage your body."

He lifted her nude body in his arms and walked to a plush rug on the floor in front of the fireplace. There was a table laden with an assortment of delicious temptations. Fresh fruits, cakes and pastries, cold chicken and a bottle of wine. The couple fed each other the foods, occasionally using a piece of food as a temptation for sampling each other's delights. Darcy laid Elizabeth back on the rug, taking some grapes in his hands, squeezed the juice on her breasts and abdomen. He lowered his head to delicately lick the juice from her body, enticing her to writhe and beg for more. Slowly, Darcy continued moving lower and lower with his tongue, until he found a thatch of chestnut curls above her most private of parts. His tongue continued to caress, as it moved into her folds, encouraging her thighs to part to welcome him. His lips and tongue took pleasure in tantalizing her, as her body ached for more. Darcy entered her with his tongue, drinking her very essence, finding the taste of her driving him further into wanton desires. Darcy then moved up, claiming her lips as his arousal claimed its home. She was made for him, so snug and fit, perfect to bring him to places he had never known. Over and over he entered her, over and over she begged for more. Their releases were brought at the same moment.

"Each time I feel as if the pleasure grows, and each time I find I want you more and more. Is this normal?" Elizabeth gasped.

"I have only the knowledge of what we have shared. Books with pictures describing different positions of making love do not speak of feelings and desires."

"Am I truly your first? I know what is said, that most men of society are...experienced." Elizabeth could not look at Darcy as she spoke.

Taking a finger, he lifted her chin and turned her face to look at him. "I have held myself for you dearest. When I was of majority, my father spoke to me quite sternly. He told me of the different men of the world, the ones who visited the certain houses in Town, the ones who kept a mistress, the ones who would defile servants. He told me that his father had given him the same talk. I was told that if I was to marry for convenience, it did not matter where I found my pleasure. But, if I was wishing for a love match, a marriage as I had witnessed in my parents' home, and that of my Aunt Elaine and Uncle Henry, I would be best to not find pleasure in any of these ways. There are ways to relieve ones self. He instructed me on these matters. But I have never had any relations with any woman until now. And I know that my father was right. I saved myself for you and have been rewarded amply for that. What you gave me in your precious gift I could not take if I could not give you the same in return. You have a part of me that no other will ever have."

Smiling sweetly, Elizabeth pulled her husband tightly to her. "I must remember to say a prayer of thanks to your father for his teachings. Your gift was indeed the most precious wedding present I could ever receive. Thank you for waiting for me. I can never tell you how dear you are to me." She snuggled close and drifted off into a peaceful sleep. Darcy lay beside her, holding her close, saying a slight thank you to his father. He was grateful he could give himself to Elizabeth, and to her alone.

The next few days were spent much the same. The couple would eat; make love, and sleep, only to repeat the acts a few hours later. They explored each other's body, discovering the preferences of the other.

The Darcy's returned to Pemberley, and this time was the formal welcome to their home for Elizabeth. The staff assembled on the front steps, awaiting the official arrival of their Mistress. Elizabeth was amazed at the sight as they arrived in their carriage. She was pleased to be able to greet the staff this time, as she only needed help because of her broken leg. Darcy was more than willing to carry his bride from the carriage to the entryway of the house, where her wheeled chair awaited her. Inside the drawing room they found the Bennets and Lord and Lady Matlock. Georgiana was practicing in the music room until she was made aware of her brother and sister being in the house. She came running to greet them.

"Elizabeth, I am so pleased to now have a sister. Welcome home. You simply glow with joy." Georgiana turned and embraced her brother. "William, welcome home. I am so pleased to see you so happy. Marriage suites you well." Darcy blushed at his sister's comment.

The other couples in the room laughed, as they were well aware of which aspect of married life suited the newlyweds well and left them glowing.

Dinner that night was a welcome home for the couple, as Georgiana had discovered Elizabeth's favorite dishes and had them fixed along with Darcy's. After the dinner, a concert was given in the music room. Darcy could see how much his sister had relaxed now that she was able to realize that Elizabeth would have all of the hostess duties from then on and that Georgiana could enjoy herself. As the family had decided that they would postpone her presentation for an extra year, Georgiana decided she wished to spend the time learning to be herself rather than what society expected of her. She also expected to learn much from her sister.

Chapter 15

The families all left Pemberley for their respective homes. Mrs. Bennet was tearfully waving goodbye to her least favorite daughter as they rode away.

Elizabeth smiled as she could imagine her mother crying about her poor nerves all the way to Longbourn and of how Elizabeth, Mary and Jane could now introduce Kitty and Lydia to other wealthy men. Darcy watched his wife's expression and lifted an eyebrow questioningly. "I can just imagine my poor father by the time they arrive home. My mother will be discussing her poor nerves all the way there and Papa will be ready to drown Mama's nerves from abusing his nerves the entire trip."

Darcy laughed and nodded as he could picture the scene. "I must take an hour in my study to see to my correspondence, would you care to bring a book in and read in front of the fire while I work?"

"I would like that very much. I will send Rebecca for my book."

"I would be agreeable in retrieving the book for my bride. There is no need for the servant to do so."

Elizabeth smiled. "What has become of the Master of Pemberley? No need of a servant to be of service to their family? How highly unusual of you my dear."

"I am more than able to climb the stairs to our chambers and retrieve a book for my beautiful wife. I will be right back, so stay put."

"I will do as commanded by the Master. I eagerly await his return." Darcy lifted his wife's hand to his lips. "What a good wife you are."

Darcy and Elizabeth settled into a routine over the next few weeks. They were both early risers, and they would go for a walk, with Darcy pushing the wheeled chair, in the gardens each morning. They would return and prepare for the day, rejoining each other's company to enjoy breakfast in the smaller breakfast room. Then they would separate, Darcy to work with his steward or other estate affairs as Elizabeth worked with Mrs. Reynolds to learn her duties and responsibilities of being Mistress. After luncheon, the couple would be together again, whether reading by the fire in his study or hidden away in their bed chambers. Evenings after dinner would be spent with Georgiana before the couple would retire early. It was not long before Georgiana would giggle as her brother and his bride made their excuses of fatigue as they retired every night.

Elizabeth had never considered using the Mistress's bedchamber for her own. She could not understand the couples whom only shared a bed once in a while to produce an heir, only to separate after their coupling to return to their own rooms. No, Darcy's bed was her bed, she would not be able to sleep anywhere else now that she had found her home in his arms. She planned on using the Mistress's bed to be used in times of great illness or when giving birth. After birthing a child, the room could be used as a temporary nursery until the child was able to sleep through the night. Elizabeth knew she would be different from her own mother in wishing to keep her child near and nurse her infant. Mrs. Bennet had always instructed her daughters that if they married well, they should employ wet nurses to nourish their infants. It was what high society families did according to what Mrs. Bennet was told.

The sitting room for the Master's suite was changed slightly as Elizabeth spent as much time in it as Darcy. There was a special book case in the room which had a shelf which could be locked. This was where certain books of a private nature were kept, for the couple to peruse at their leisure. A second desk was brought into the sitting room for Elizabeth's use. This room was commonly used by the couple in the late afternoon, as they grew quite fond of the rug in front of the fireplace.

Elizabeth's dressing room had begun to fill as all of items of her trousseau arrived. Another arrival was shocking to Elizabeth, as Darcy had ordered a special wedding gift for her, though in actuality, they would both enjoy it. It was a new bathing tub, large enough for three people to sit in. A deep blush covered Elizabeth's face as she saw the tub for the first time. She had many possibilities running through her mind of the uses of this tub.

It was nearly July when Doctor Woodland gave Elizabeth a clean bill of health, removing her splint from her leg. She was told to use a cane for a few weeks as she built up the strength in the leg after so long of no use. For the first few days after the splint was removed, Darcy insisted on continuing to carry her, especially when it came to the staircase. After the first day, Elizabeth decided that her husband needed to control his worrying and she told him so in a kind but stern manner. The first time she walked up the stairs alone, her husband stood at the bottom of the stairs biting his lip as he nervously watched.

Now that Elizabeth was healed and able to use her leg, new methods of lovemaking were discovered and employed vigorously. They also did not restrict their coupling to just their bedchamber. Many of the servants of Pemberley's main house were shocked as their formerly stoic and somber master was now found coming from different locations of the house, usually in a disheveled appearance, pulling behind him his wife, who was equally disheveled in appearance. Mrs. Reynolds could only laugh. She was quite pleased with seeing her master finally happy and behaving like a young boy rather than the young man who had been forced to carry so much grown up responsibility at such a young age. He had lost so many years of his youth when he had to take of control of Pemberley at the tender age of two and twenty, and having to care for his young sister. Darcy would never have complained about taking on so much responsibility at such an age when most men were looking forward to meeting young ladies during Season, going to balls, and frolicking around enjoying themselves.

But now was Darcy's time to enjoy himself. And Mrs. Reynolds was quite grateful for his finding Elizabeth.

Fall meant harvest time and Darcy would be busy day after day as he was in the fields with his steward. Elizabeth tried to prepare for this as she knew that she would miss her husband's presence throughout the day. She planned to spend time reading, writing to her mother and father, and sharing time with her new sister. One afternoon, the second week of October, Elizabeth decided to go for a horse ride with Georgiana. Elizabeth was not near the horse rider that either of the siblings were, but under her new sister's tutelage she was improving daily.

The pair decided to ride to the lake on the estate, and would enjoy a picnic on the shores. Elizabeth had brought a book with her to read after they ate. She had also received several letters that day from her family and wished to read them while she was relaxing.

"Oh, Georgiana, you will be so surprised when you hear this. My parents are spending more time together, even taking walks together while holding hands. Kitty is quite amazed and says that Mama has calmed considerably. She no longer has fits of nerves and has even spoken to both of my sisters about their behaving in a calmer manner. My heavens, I wonder where my mother has disappeared to. Or maybe Papa is putting brandy into her eggs at breakfast." Both ladies laughed. "Oh, I have a letter from Jane. She says that William invited them to come next month so that he can take Charles around to some of the estates that would be available for purchase. This would be pleasant, having Jane nearby such as Mary is. Especially now, as Mary is expecting."

Elizabeth and Darcy had been told the previous week of the expectant addition to their family. Fitzwilliam was a bundle of excitement, treating his wife as if she was a china doll who might shatter at the slightest touch. Darcy laughed at his cousin, the man who had been a colonel in the regulars and survived many wars was all nerves about becoming a father.

Darcy turned to Elizabeth and smiled. "And you say I am a mother hen. Look at my cousin."

Elizabeth laughed as she remembered Fitzwilliam fluttering around her sister.

As the sisters were relaxing and talking about Mary and Fitzwilliam, they did not hear the approaching danger lurking behind a tree nearby. Wickham had determined his revenge, and had waited patiently for his chance to strike. He had been in the area for several days, after learning of the habits of the two ladies. He had a very willing and unwitting accomplice in the very naïve Lydia Bennet. When he learned of the ladies enjoying afternoon rides while Darcy was working with the harvest, Wickham knew he had the perfect solution to exact his pound of flesh from the man he despised.

Wickham quietly crept forward until he was nearly able to touch Georgiana. "Good afternoon, Ladies." Wickham declared with a very wicked grin. "It is a pleasure to find you here. I have missed both of you ladies dearly. Both of you were taken from me by the same man, now it is my turn to repay his kindness." Georgiana quickly moved to her sister, as Elizabeth pushed the young girl behind her.

"What are you doing here, Mr. Wickham? You are not welcome here at Pemberley."

"I missed my childhood home. I, also, miss my bride who was taken from me before I had the pleasure of branding her mine. And you, Mrs. Darcy, I was becoming quite fond of you as well. How dare Darcy rob me of all three?"

"William never robbed you of any of it. You robbed yourself of all you wished for, because of your greed and desires. You signed away your right to the living left to you by Mr. Darcy. And I was told you received generous compensation for it. You never loved Georgiana, only her dowry. Gratefully my husband was able to stop your plans before it was too late. She was a child, believing your romantic tale of love. But it was love of money, not her. I may have thought you interesting when we first met, but have come to know the real scoundrel you are, and am quite pleased that I did not allow your lies to convince me to refuse William."

"But, Miss Lydia told me you did refuse Darcy at first. She said that you stood up to him concerning his treatment of me. Is that not so?"

"I was angry over other matters and only made statements when I did not know the whole story. Once I did, I eagerly accepted William and have not regretted it for a moment." Elizabeth could feel Georgiana shaking behind her, leaning closely to her body. "Now I will ask again, why are you here?"

"I wish to reclaim what should have been mine. Darcy ruined my chance of marital bliss with your young sister. When I thought I might have a chance with a country beauty such as you, Darcy again ruined my chances. I only wish to repay him for his actions." Wickham pulled out a gun and leveled it at Elizabeth. "Now, here is some rope. Georgiana, I want you to take the rope and tie your sister's hands together. And remember, I am watching you. Do not attempt to escape, or one of you will be shot immediately."

Elizabeth coaxed her sister from behind her and told her to do as Wickham demanded. "It will be alright Georgiana, do as you are told."

Georgiana cautiously moved towards Wickham, taking the rope from his hand. She began to wrap the rope around Elizabeth's wrists, leaving them loose. Suddenly she received a smack across her face from Wickham. "I told you not to attempt to escape. Now, tie her hands tightly. I wish to see that the ropes are cutting into her tender flesh Georgiana, or I will put a bullet in your dear sister and leave her here. Which would you prefer?"

"It is fine Georgiana, do as he says. You will not hurt me, for I know it was Wickham's doing which would injure me." Elizabeth looked at the quivering girl, knowing how deeply frightened she was.

Georgiana finally secured Elizabeth's wrists, and then wrapped her arms around her sister. "I am so sorry Elizabeth. Please forgive me."

"I told you, there is nothing to forgive you for. This is Wickham's doing."

"Now, Elizabeth, lie on the ground, on your stomach. Do it now, or I will shoot Georgie here."

"What are you planning? I will do as you ask if you tell me what you plan."

"I plan to secure little sister there, and place her on her horse. Then I will secure you to your horse. We will leave here together, travelling to a place I have ready for our enjoyment." The leer on his face led Elizabeth to fear of his intentions. She knew that if they were taken to this location, Wickham would certainly defile both of them.

Elizabeth began to lie down, which caught Wickham's attention. As he was looking at her, planning what pleasures he would take of her body, he was not paying close enough attention to Georgiana. Elizabeth had noticed the girl's location near the horses, with Elizabeth between her and Wickham. When she felt Wickham was completely occupied with his thoughts of defiling Mrs. Darcy, Elizabeth yelled to her sister. "Run, Georgiana, run. Get away."

Wickham ran forward to grab the young girl, only to wind up on the ground from Elizabeth kicking him. Georgiana froze, trying to decide what to do. She did not wish to leave Elizabeth, and yet wished to run as far as possible from Wickham. "Georgiana, go, get help. I am fine, go for help. Hurry."

Georgiana finally collected herself from her fears and jumped onto the horse, racing off towards Pemberley. Wickham shouted for her to come back, and he continued to struggle with Elizabeth who was fighting him.

When Georgiana was quite a distance away, she heard a sound which chilled her to the bone. There was a single gunshot which seemed to echo though Georgiana's mind. Tears were streaming down her face when she spotted several men riding towards her on horseback. One of the men was none other than her brother.

"Georgiana, are you well? Where is Elizabeth? What has happened? Was Wickham here?" Georgiana was having difficulties finding her voice. She nodded at the last question and pointed towards the lake. "Go back to the house and have someone sent for the constable. Send for Doctor Woodland as well. Now, go, Georgiana. I wish for you to be safe." He motioned for one of the men to accompany his sister while the other would go with him.

Georgiana and the hand who was riding with her arrived at the main house, and they were met by Mrs. Reynolds. A report had reached the house earlier that Wickham had been seen and she had sent word to Darcy in the fields. Mrs. Reynolds also sent the information that the ladies were out riding, she thought towards the lake. Another hand was sent to Lambton for the constable and for Doctor Woodland. Word spread quickly through the estate of Wickham being there and his attack on the ladies. It was still unknown if Elizabeth was well or if Darcy had located her and saved her from Wickham. No one knew, at this point, if the gunshot which had rung out had hit its intended target.

As Doctor Woodland arrived, a fast moving rider came to a screeching halt at the front steps. It was Fitzwilliam who had heard of his sister and cousin being in jeopardy at the hands of Wickham. He asked where Darcy and Elizabeth were and Mrs. Reynolds told him they were last seen in the direction of the lake. Fitzwilliam jumped back on his horse, and yelled to the housekeeper to send someone to his home to retrieve Mary.

Fitzwilliam sped as fast as his horse could run towards the lake. As he grew near the shores, he saw several horses coming towards him. There was a body lying across the saddle of one of the horses, a man's body as the boots stuck out from under the blanket which was covering the body. Fitzwilliam then became aware of his cousin who was clutching Elizabeth to his chest as they rode on his horse. They rode up beside Fitzwilliam and he looked under the blanket to see that the body was of Wickham. Darcy shook his head, wishing to get Elizabeth to the house before he spoke of the event.

Chapter 16

The group continued to the main house, and were met by the constable riding to meet them. He, too, was able to see the body and the way Darcy held his wife. Knowing the Master of Pemberley well, he followed the group to the house before being able to question the group.

When they arrived at the house, Darcy carried his wife straight into the infirmary. "William, I will be fine. Please, we need to speak with the constable. Then I wish to go up to our room."

"Dearest, indulge me in this. I wish the doctor to ensure me that you are well. Please, my love, allow me this reassurance."

Elizabeth placed a hand on the side of her husband's face. "For you, my love, and only to put you at ease." He took her hand and placed a kiss in her palm.

As Doctor Woodland took Georgiana into the infirmary so he could evaluate each of the Darcy ladies, Darcy stepped into the drawing room where the constable and Fitzwilliam were waiting. "Mr. Darcy, your cousin has just confirmed to me that the body across the horse outside is indeed as I suspected, George Wickham. Can you tell me just what has occurred here today?"

"Mr. Winters, please take a seat. You too, Richard. May I offer either of you a drink, this will take a little while."

Both men accepted a glass of port and took a seat. "I was working in the fields with my steward when an urgent message was sent to me from Mrs. Reynolds alerting me that Wickham had been seen lurking around the estate. I was also informed that my wife and sister were riding towards the lake for a picnic. I brought two hands with me and raced towards the lake. On our way, we found Georgiana riding away from the lake, crying hard and she pointed us to where

Wickham and Elizabeth had last been seen. I sent Georgiana and one of the hands to come to the house and request for you and Doctor Woodland be summoned to the estate. The other hand and I rode on as quickly as we could. When we arrived at the shores of the lake, my heart stopped. Elizabeth was lying on the ground on her back with Wickham lying on top of her. Her eyes were closed and I feared the worse. When she heard us approaching, she opened her eyes. I jumped down and ran to her, pushing Wickham from her body. It was then I saw blood covering Elizabeth's dress. She began telling me she was fine, that it was not her blood. I realized that the blood was Wickham's. They had struggled for the gun when Georgiana ran at Elizabeth's orders, and when the gun went off, it was into Wickham's chest. He died almost instantly."

Fitzwilliam was shocked at the events. "How did he find them? Did he harm them in any way before his death?"

Darcy shook his head. "Elizabeth said that he held the gun pointed at her, demanding Georgiana to bind Elizabeth's hands. When Georgiana did so leaving the rope loose, Wickham struck her across her face. He demanded she tie the rope tightly as to cut into Elizabeth's flesh or Wickham would shoot one of them. Elizabeth told Georgiana to do as he said, and after it was done, Wickham demanded Elizabeth lie on the ground. When Wickham's attention was on her, she yelled to my sister to run. Wickham moved to stop Georgiana only to find Elizabeth kicking him and knocking him to the ground. Even with her hands tied, she fought Wickham until his gun discharged. She was worried about Georgiana's safety when we arrived. Once she knew that Georgiana was well, Elizabeth was able to let down her defenses and began to feel the fear she had been struggling against since the first moment she spied Wickham."

Fitzwilliam was furious, and if Wickham was not already dead, he would have killed him with his bare hands. "He can no longer harm our family. May he rest in hell." Fitzwilliam spat out as he clinched his fists. Mr. Winters agreed. "Well, Mr. Darcy, I would like to speak with both of the ladies separately, and if they tell me the same information, there is no reason to deal with this blackguard any further."

"If you would be so kind as to wait for the doctor to finish his examinations, I would be grateful."

"Of course. Their welfare is the most important issue at the moment. They have been through so much today." A knock on the door announced the arrival of Mary. Fitzwilliam stood and hurried across the room to his wife, telling her only the briefest of information before sending her to be with her sister. He would tell her more of the story later.

Nearly an hour passed before Doctor Woodland came to the drawing room. The constable remained in the room as the doctor described the conditions of his patients. Georgiana had bruising and swelling across the right side of her face, where she was smacked. There was also a cut which was cleaned and should heal with no difficulties. Elizabeth had cuts on both of her wrists from the rope. She also had some burns on her right hand from the powder of the gun, as the gun was trapped between her and Wickham. I am more concerned with Mrs. Darcy's emotional state. She has been through an ordeal which would make most men cringe. We will need to be patient and caring as she comes to terms with what has happened."

"May I speak with her for a few moments, Doctor? I will be very brief."

"Very brief, for I need to give her a draught to aid her in some sleep." The constable nodded. "I feel Miss Darcy would also benefit from a draught if you will agree, Mr. Darcy."

"I agree with you. My sister was distraught when I saw her on the road. She will be in need of help to deal with what she witnessed. Does she know of Wickham's demise?"

"Mrs. Darcy has told her. I would like to keep both of the ladies downstairs for the evening. May we put Mrs. Darcy in the room across the hallway from the infirmary and Miss Darcy in the infirmary?"

"Mrs. Reynolds, will you see that this is handled?" A nod came from his housekeeper as she hurried off to make the preparations. "Which of my ladies would you prefer to speak with first?" Darcy inquired of the constable.

"I think that Mrs. Darcy would probably be best at the moment. Hopefully, I will not need to disturb Miss Darcy."

"Let me lead you to my wife." Fitzwilliam followed after the other men, and as they entered the guest room, Fitzwilliam entered the infirmary to see a sobbing Georgiana grasping Mary for comfort. Fitzwilliam walked over and sat on the edge of the bed where Georgiana lay, and he placed a hand on her shoulder. Georgiana had not noticed her cousin had entered the room. When she looked up to see who was next to her, her sobs became stronger as she saw the man who shared guardianship over her with her brother.

"Georgiana, how are you dearest? Do you require anything?"

"Richard, I am so very ashamed. I should never have listened to Wickham's lies, and I should never have rode off and left Elizabeth alone with him, with her hands tightly bound. It is all my fault. Elizabeth was stronger than I, she was able to fight him while I ran away."

"From what I have been told, Elizabeth yelled to you to leave and get help. You did as she asked you to, you were able to break away and find your brother, sending him in the correct direction. I am proud of you Georgiana. Darcy was able to locate Elizabeth quicker because of you. And Elizabeth told how you were forced to bind her hands, but that you tied the rope loose at first. You paid the price for that by being smacked across the face, which I see the result on the side of your face as we speak. Only when Elizabeth told you it was alright, did you do as Wickham demanded by binding her hands tightly. You fought back in a way, only giving in when you feared Wickham using his gun to kill you or Elizabeth. Georgiana, I am very proud of you. You defied Wickham. You defended your sister. Thank the heavens that you both survived relatively unscathed."

Georgiana continued to sob, though it was becoming less intense. Mary had only been told bits and pieces, but as she began to grasp the entire story, horror was written across her expression. "Georgiana, the doctor will be back in a moment with a draught for you. He says you need to rest."

"Mary, I am fine. My face has a bruise on it and a small cut. Otherwise I am fine. It is Elizabeth I am concerned about. What she had to endure, oh, I just know she is hurt worse than she is letting me know."

"Georgiana, will you believe me if I check on my sister and tell you what I discover? You know that I will not lie to you, for I am just as concerned for my sister."

"I will trust what you tell me Mary." Mary nodded and left the room, leaving her husband to console his young cousin. It was not long before she returned with a smile on her face. "Lizzy is doing quite well. She is even adamant about sleeping in her own bed tonight. Only when William threatened to tie her to the bed to win her compliance did she finally give in to the doctor's orders. The constable just left and Doctor Woodland just gave Elizabeth a draught. He says that she will be asleep in a few moments and then he would come over to give you something as well. Other than some cuts from the ropes, which she has told me to relay to you was not your doing but from her fighting Wickham, and a slight burn on her hand, she is unharmed."

"Are you telling me everything? Please do not hide anything from me. I heard gun fire, I know you are not telling me something."

"Georgiana, I will tell you what your brother told me. When he arrived at the location, Elizabeth was lying on the ground with Wickham on top of her. The gunshot you heard occurred when Elizabeth was struggling with Wickham, the gun was between them as they were fighting and with the barrel pointed at Wickham, the trigger was pulled and

Wickham was killed. He was on top of her when it happened and his body held her to the ground. Because they were so close when the gun went off, there were powder burns on Lizzy's hand. That is all."

Mary was nodding as she listened to her husband. "She is relieved to know you are well, and that Wickham did not do as he had planned. From what she said, it is obvious he planned to violate both of you to exact revenge against William. Now, Georgiana, we have told you what we know, and there is nothing being hidden from you. When the doctor comes, please take the draught and get some sleep. We will stay here in case you need us."

Chapter 17

Elizabeth woke in the middle of the night, as a nightmare stole into her mind. She could see Wickham's sneer, his desire to accost both her and Georgiana. She could feel his hands running over her body as he tried to force himself on her. Georgiana lay on the ground nearby, blood running down her face as she was unconscious. When she woke, she found her husband's arms wrapped securely around her. He felt her sit up quickly and sat up beside her. His arms were still wrapped around her and he pulled her possessively to his body. "It was a nightmare dearest, you are fine. All will be well. Shall I send for another draught for you? The doctor says you need to sleep."

"No, I am well. I would prefer being here in your arms. It will take some time, I just need to be safe in your embrace."

"Would you care to talk about the nightmare?"

"It is just the way Wickham looked at us. He had intended on defiling us. He admitted so. The way he glared, he made my skin crawl without even touching me."

Darcy shuddered at the thought of such a man even daring to look at either of the women who were most important in his life, let alone Wickham stating designs to touch them in such a vulgar way. He could understand why Elizabeth continued to shake as she spoke. "He will never be able to touch you again. You are safe my love."

"I killed him. I ended his life." Elizabeth looked into her husband's eyes, tears flowing down her face.

"Lizzy, he was trying to kill you. In your struggle to save your own life, the gun discharged. You did not intend on causing his death, no matter how vile his was. You were fighting for your own life. It is unfortunate that you had to struggle with him, but you did not kill him. He ended his own life. His greed and lechery lead to his demise, not you."

"William, I need to remove him from my mind. I need to replace the memories of his sneer and harshness with memories of your kindness and love. Please make love to me. Push the day's events from my mind, and give me the most pleasant of memories to replace the pain. I need you, inside me, loving me."

"Are you certain that it is truly what you desire?" Darcy wished for nothing more, but feared taking advantage of her.

"I want you. I want the man I love to love me, brand me his, make my mind and body writhe with pleasure. Please, William, I need you to love me."

No further pleading was necessary.

The following morning after the attack Georgiana was still quite shaken from her experience. The doctor decided it would be wise for her to have another draught and sleep longer. When she woke the next time, he advised that it would be best for Elizabeth to be with her alone first, for Elizabeth could speak to her of what they had shared in during the experience. Darcy did not wish for the ladies to endure this alone, but Doctor Woodland was adamant that each of the ladies would heal much quicker by discussing their impressions of what happened.

Several hours later, Georgiana woke with her sister at her side. "Welcome back, Georgiana. How are you?"

"Elizabeth, I am pleased that you are here, for I am not sure I could bear to have one of the others comforting me."

"What you witnessed was horrifying, and only you can determine the best way for you to recover. I have begun to heal in my own way with the help of your brother. He was kind, but it was when I needed him to do as I requested without question, William did not hesitate to give me this chance to heal. Now, Georgiana, what do you need from all of us to allow you to begin to heal?"

"I feel so guilty for what occurred. If I had not believed Wickham when we were at Ramsgate and agreed to run off with him, he might not have decided to seek revenge."

Elizabeth shook her head. "I have learned so much from speaking with others in regards to Wickham's behaviors. I have determined that no matter what you had done; Wickham would have found another way to strike out at William. He was bitter and jealous of William. Your father was kind to Wickham, some believe out of sympathy when Wickham's father, who had been a devoted servant for many years, died. Wickham twisted your father's gifts into his own version. In his mind, he saw your father's gifts as your father desiring him to be heir to Pemberley."

"Wickham saw your father as wishing for someone to replace William as his heir. This delusion drove Wickham further and further into his desire to strike out at William. I met Wickham when he was in the militia and staying near Meryton. He told me stories of being harmed by William, not of your near elopement, of William denying the living your father had left him and how William was bitter because your father had loved Wickham best. At the time I was foolishly wishing to believe the worst of your brother. This is one of the accusations I made at your brother when he first proposed to me. William was not very elegant in his proposal, and I took offense to it. I wished to strike back at him, and I accused him of purposely harming Wickham. The letter which I am sure by now you are aware that your brother gave me, I had just finished reading when the storm struck and changed my life forever, told me of Wickham's history with your family and his betrayal."

"I never knew of any betrayal. What did he do?"

"From what I understand, he would purposely do things to harm William, constantly placing William's life in jeopardy. He would break things, ruin things, and then always blame William.

Wickham purposely tried to make your good brother appear unworthy of his inheritance and tried desperately to dispose of William in an effort to be heir to Pemberley. Wickham knew that no matter what he did, William would never tell of his evil. William did not wish to hurt your father, and he continued this much ingrained behavior long after your father's death. It was only last spring when I made accusations against William that he finally allowed himself to begin to speak of the betrayal."

"I never knew. I thought William and Wickham had always been friends. I am so ashamed, that of all the people I could have allowed to fool me, it would be the one who despised my dear brother. However can he forgive me for behaving so?"

"Because William realized that Wickham tried to seduce a child, you were not a woman who was prepared for the world. Wickham took advantage of the situation. The fact he found you attractive was a bonus to him. He knew that William would never reveal the truth, for William never had before. You were vulnerable, and Wickham took advantage of that. Do you know why you chose to accept Wickham's advances when you knew it was a break in propriety?"

"I was lonely. I have thought of it many times, and realized that I was very lonely. Father was devoted to me and we spent so much time together. I loved Father and his death took away the one man I knew dearly loved me. William was busy learning the estate business and growing into his role. He was too busy to spend time with me. I think, in his own way, it was how he dealt with his grief. So, when Wickham was kind and attentive to me, I was thrilled for the opportunity to have companionship. It was only later that I learned of his desire to steal my dowry. And I learned of my former companion's assisting him. I had never felt lonelier. I am shocked to learn of the years of anguish which William suffered, he never showed it. If I had known, I would never have allowed Wickham's attentions towards me."

"I believe that it was a very hard lesson for your brother to learn. But, now he knows what his silence nearly cost him. It nearly robbed him of his beloved sister and her happiness. It, also, nearly robbed him of me. Only when he told me the truth was he able to show me the true Fitzwilliam Darcy. And I am so very pleased that he did. To think I nearly lost the chance to marry the best of men because I believed the lies of a horrible man. I am pleased that William chose to give me another chance. I love him so very dearly and would have regretted his loss the rest of my life if he had not."

"Elizabeth, thank you for telling me this. I wish I had known it years ago. I understand so many things better now. May I have some time alone to think?"

"Of course. And if you wish to speak further of this, know that I am here for you. I also believe that, though difficult for him to speak of it, William would be willing to answer questions if you had any for him."

Georgiana embraced her sister, thanking her for the information which opened Georgiana's mind to so much. Things from the past, Wickham's words at different times, all began to take on a new light. She knew that William was the type to remain quiet, but she was amazed that she would protect such a man for the sake of their father.

Nearly an hour later, William knocked on the infirmary door and was welcomed inside. "How are you, dearest? Would you like some food?"

"Not quite yet. I would appreciate a moment of your time though."

"Of course, Georgiana." He walked forward, and sat himself on the side of the bed, taking one of her hands in his. "What is it you wish to discuss?"

"Elizabeth told me how you spent your life protecting Wickham's reputation and cleaning up his messes. Why would you do so? Especially after Father died. There was no need to protect Wickham in Father's eyes any longer."

Darcy looked into his sister's young eyes. "By the time Father died, it was engrained in me to protect Wickham's reputation. I am not quite sure I was aware I was doing it because I did so naturally for so many years. Father would have been devastated to know how he wasted all of his attention on Wickham. If he would have known all the pain Wickham would inflict on so many people, Father would never have bestowed such kindness on the boy Wickham."

"I think Father would be proud of you. You are truly the best of men. I am pleased that you did not lose Elizabeth because of Wickham's lies. You deserve the happiness you have with her, and you deserve to be loved." Georgiana smiled and embraced her brother. "I am pleased to have such a wonderful brother, as well as a loving new sister."

Darcy knew that his wife had aided his sister to the road of recovery. How had he ever lived his life before Elizabeth Bennet Darcy entered it? He knew what a precious gift she was and was grateful everyday that she read the letter he wrote.

Chapter 18

The Bingleys arrived the second week of November and were to stay at Pemberley for a fortnight. Darcy had been informed of six estates in the county which were available to purchase. He knew each estate, and could answer most questions Bingley would have. Appointments were made each day to visit the different estates, with the husbands viewing books and speaking with stewards. The wives spoke with the housekeepers and viewed the rooms of each house.

The fifth estate was the one which won the Bingleys. The estate was Mooring Park. It was located on the other side of Fitzwilliam's estate, with a large property. The house was pleasant, the rooms were well situated, large and airy. The furnishing and wall coverings were dated, but in good condition. The previous owner had died ten years before but the family had only recently desired to sell the estate. The price was in Bingley's range, as well, the income from the estate would be nearly six thousand per annum, an increase from Bingley's normal five thousand. The furnishings and wall coverings could be replaced at the couple's leisure, saving them the immediate cost. The sisters were thrilled they would be so close, as it would allow the families to spend much time together. The Bingleys had been living in London since the wedding, as they had given up the lease at Netherfield. Jane was use to the country, and though she was not the avid walker as Elizabeth, Jane grew tired of London and the lack of freedom the city did not offer.

A celebration dinner was planned, and an invitation was sent to Fitzwilliam and Mary to join them. Mary was nearly four months into her pregnancy, and her husband was continuing his overprotective nature. This made for much teasing, as the men commented about the man before them formerly leading leagues of soldiers into battle and yet was so fragile about his wife being with child. The women laughed and commented that once the child was born, Fitzwilliam would have to order new rugs and boots as he was bound to wear them out with his pacing in his nervousness. The baby was due near the couple's first wedding anniversary, and would keep them from going to London during the Season. Mary was pleased with this prospect as she had been nervous about her mother in law's determination of showing off her new daughter.

Lady Matlock was so pleased with her daughter that she was constantly planning dinners and other ways to introduce Mary to everyone. Now that Mary was carrying the first grandchild, Lady Matlock was beside herself with joy.

The Bingley's would move into their new home near Christmas. The families had all been invited to Pemberley for the holiday season, and most were coming. The Gardiners were unable to attend due to Mr. Gardiner's work. Lydia was travelling to Brighton to spend the holidays with her friend, Mrs. Forrester. Lydia was not easily welcome at Pemberley after it was discovered she had spoken with Wickham after her father had told her to stay away from the man, giving him information which aided him in his attack on Elizabeth and Georgiana. Darcy could not easily forgive such behavior, and Elizabeth had grown tired of her youngest sister's inability to behave properly.

Christmas had been a quiet affair since the death of Darcy's parents. Normally, besides church service, the siblings only exchanged a few gifts and shared a nice meal together. Georgiana was known to play a small concert for her brother as part of her gift to him. This year, the old decorations were brought down from the attic, a tree was cut and brought into the grand ballroom and decorated. Elizabeth and Georgiana collaborated as to new traditions they wished to start. They requested holly and ivy collected to be draped throughout the house, and a kissing bough, which Elizabeth planned to put to good use was placed in the drawing room. There would be sleigh rides for those who wished to venture into the snow which was already beginning to pile higher than Elizabeth had ever seen in Hertfordshire. Being so much further to the south, Elizabeth's childhood home had a calmer claim on the weather. In Derbyshire, there were days when one could not venture out of doors because of the extreme conditions.

These were the days when Elizabeth was to spend hidden away with her handsome husband. She would pretend they were alone in the honeymoon cottage, just the two of them exploring each other's delights. No one came to the house claiming need to discuss issues with the Master of Pemberley, as no one dared step out of doors unless there was an extreme need on those days. Darcy, realizing his beloved was use to being able to traipse through the park of Hertfordshire, even in the winter, decided to give his wife an early Christmas gift. He knew in the fall that there would be a great adjustment for his bride to become accustomed to, and he began his plan with his head gardener. They prepared to turn the Mistress's bedchamber into a small and very private park. In the hot house, the gardener prepared by potting several small trees, many pots of flowering plants, and plants which were commonly kept indoors of grand homes. They had, also, collected many palm sized stones, which would be used to create a small path in the private park.

Before the family members descended upon them, Darcy put his plan in motion. As he kept Elizabeth occupied in his study with plans, his staff began to make the transformation. When Darcy was requested to give his opinion, Mrs. Reynolds came to speak to Elizabeth to finalize the plans for the holiday menus. After dinner, Darcy claimed he was greatly exhausted and wished to retire early. Elizabeth was surprised and somewhat concerned, as her husband rarely begged not to spend a few hours with his sister. "Are you well?" Elizabeth asked as she placed a hand on his cheek to check for a fever. Darcy nodded. "I am perfect. I have a Christmas gift which I wish to give you early and in private." He took his wife's hand and led her upstairs. He had Rebecca waiting in the dressing room for her Mistress, and he took her to the door from the hallway to the dressing room.

"I will come for you in half an hour. Do not leave this room until I come for you." Darcy smiled and placed a light kiss on his wife's lips. Elizabeth had a curious expression on her face as she agreed to behave and wait in the dressing room for him.

Rebecca could not wipe the smile she wore from her face which only added to

Elizabeth's curiosity. The half hour seemed to take forever, but finally there was a knock on the door followed by Darcy entering the room. Rebecca knew it was her time to disappear until she was rung for the next day. Darcy walked up behind Elizabeth who was seated in front of the mirror, as Rebecca had just been brushing her hair.

"As I wish for your present to be a surprise, I must blindfold you to take you to it."

"William, whatever are you planning?"

Darcy smiled sheepishly and shook his head. "As you are to discover it in moments, I will not ruin the surprise right now. You must do as I ask." Looking at her husband's expression brought a giggle to Elizabeth. "I will do as I am requested, Mr. Darcy. Blindfold me and take me away." She declared as she closed her eyes in preparation.

Darcy gently tied a silken handkerchief around his beloved wife's eyes, then took her by the hand and led her to their private oasis of paradise. As they stepped into the next room, Elizabeth could feel the rocks under her feet and was surprised. When they reached what Elizabeth thought to be the center of the Mistress bedchamber, Darcy removed the blindfold. Elizabeth gasped with delight at the change in the room. The trees were small, but along with the other plants in the room gave the feeling of a wooded park. Green fabric had been draped on the walls as well as on the floor. The bed frame had been removed and the bed itself was hidden on the floor under green sheets. They walked to the bed, and Darcy gently lowered his love to the cushioning.

"Oh, William. It is like being out in the park in spring. And we are making love in our private park. This is indeed a blessed gift. I will forever treasure that you did this. But it must have taken a very long time to prepare."

"And are you not amazed at how busy we kept you all day today? I have had the staff planning this for months, and while I kept you busy, the staff quickly put the plan into action. When I was needed, Mrs. Reynolds was employed to occupy you. She was surprised that you would be so willing and kind to go over the menu as you had already made final decisions on them days ago. But it was the only idea she could come up with, which would keep you in the study."

"This is so amazing. I feel like it is spring, and I am in the park near Longbourn. I cannot imagine a more perfect gift. Thank you so very much." She continued to look around the room at the many special touches that were placed in the room. "I have often dreamed of loving you in a green meadow."

Darcy began to slip her night dress off her shoulder as he kissed her neck. "I am here to please you my love. Here to bring you a piece of heaven that is only for us." He released one of her breasts as his lips traveled to enjoy the soft moans that came from his wife as he suckled her voluptuous mounds. He continued to caress her nipples as his mouth traveled up to her mouth, devouring her lips and drinking deeply of her. Her hands roamed over his back, then moved forward to the buttons restraining his bulging arousal. He was so very thrilled with her response to the room, as he too had dreamed of making love to her in a meadow. They were in their own world, one of his making, and he found her quite delicious.

As the buttons were released, her hands entered inside his trousers, massaging and caressing him in such a way that he nearly lost his control. No, this was her gift, and he was planning to proceed to bring her the utmost pleasure. One of his hands inched its way downward, caressing its way towards her pleasure. Once at the thatch of chestnut curls, he caressed light circles in the curls and then into her folds. Her legs spread to give him access. Darcy left her lips to enjoy his pleasure of drinking in her essence, his tongue tantalizing her pearl. Elizabeth arched towards him, her legs wrapped around his shoulders, as if to hold him there, spreading wider to allow him further access as his tongue entered into her lush confines. His tongue plunged into her over and over, causing her to reach a very powerful peak.

As he prepared to remove his trousers to enter her, Elizabeth surprised her husband. "William, let me assist you. Lie on your back, allow me to do the work."

Seeing as this was his gift to her and he wished to give her pleasure, he decided to allow her to decide how it was to be conducted. He lay back on the soft mattress, with the smooth silk beneath his skin. Elizabeth pulled his trousers off, tossing them to the side where he had disposed of her night dress when he began his seduction of her. She started caressing his manhood, making him harden from her touch. She climbed on top of her husband, taking him inside her, moving slowly up and down, allowing his entry to be slow and exquisitely beautiful. He shuddered with each entrance, as her tight confines continued to caress his essence from him. His moans were low and long, bringing her a very pleased smile. She sat on top of him, moving over and over, as his hands reached forward to tease her breasts. Soon Elizabeth began to build faster and faster into a rhythm as his hips rose to enter her further and further. Her long seduction of him reached a fevered pitch as he spilt his seed inside her and she found yet another peak herself before collapsing on top of him, as they remained connected.

"My dear Lizzy, this was to be your gift, and yet you managed to give me one even greater." Darcy said as he gasped for breath. "What a truly generous woman you are." His arms were wrapped around her tightly, with his head resting against her hair. "Do you like your Christmas present?"

"No, William, I do not like my present." Elizabeth turned her eyes up towards him as he frowned. "I dearly love it. It is so very perfect. My gift to you will pale in comparison."

"Any gift you give me is a treasure to me. And remember, I am finding much pleasure in this gift as you are." He smiled to her, placing a light kiss on her forehead as he reached for the counterpane to pull over them. "So when am I to receive my gift? Do I have to behave until Christmas morning and unwrap it before the family?"

Elizabeth had an impish grin as she rolled off her husband and onto her side. "I would not wish for you to unwrap your gift in front of my family for I would be deeply embarrassed if you did." Darcy was intrigued by the look on her face.

"If that is so, when do I receive my gift?" She took his hand and slid it over her breasts, then down to a slight swell in her abdomen. There was a flutter from inside her which made his eyes grow wide with wonder. "Is it...is that...are you sure...am I...?"

"Do you like your gift? Yes, dearest, you are going to be a father. I felt the quickening this very morning, but you kept me so busy all day I had no chance to tell you."

"My dearest, I am so pleased. I am also pleased you were able to tell me here and now. Yes, yes, yes. I am going to be a father!" Darcy was literally shouting his delight. "Are you well, is everything good?" He began his mother hen position immediately as Elizabeth suspected he would.

With a laugh, Elizabeth nodded her head. "I spoke with the midwife this morning after I felt the quickening."

"How is it that I did not notice the changes in your body that are now very obvious to me? When will our child arrive? I will have to hire the doctor to move in here the month before the baby is due and have nurses and midwives available around the clock. When do we need to interview wet nurses? The nursery, we need to start immediately to prepare the nursery. It will need to be completely redone, as there have been no children in it since Georgiana was a baby. There are so many plans to make, oh my, which should be done first?"

Taking her husband's face in her hands, Elizabeth continued to laugh at him. "Dearest, we have plenty of time. I am only three months along. Our baby will arrive near the first week of June. We have no need to rush, especially in hiring a wet nurse. I plan to nurse our children. I know that it is not the fashionable thing, but I cannot imagine our baby taking nourishment from another woman."

"We will discuss that later. For now, I will concentrate on the nursery. And your care, that is the most important issue for me. I will be very attentive to everything, please forgive me for my protectiveness. I know I will be overwhelming at times, but I am so very concerned with your welfare. Please do not ask me to change, as I will not. My mother died in childbirth and it nearly killed my father to lose her. I will do everything in my power to protect you from harm. You have had enough this past year to deal with. Please bear with me, for I so dearly love you."

"I understand William, and I will be understanding for now. But remember that I am not a china doll. I am in good health, my mother gave birth to five healthy children with no difficulties and I am in better condition than she was. I am sure that I will be fine as will our child. But I do understand your fears from your own mother's loss. I will not argue if you choose to hire staff to be here for my health, but I draw the line at being carried around in a cart by four footmen." This brought a laugh from her husband.

"I will cross that off the list I have started in my mind. A child. My child. Lizzy, you are truly amazing. Thank you my beautiful and enchanting wife. Thank you for making me a father."

He kissed her over and over, making her giggle with delight.

Mrs. Reynolds heard from several of the servants of the shouts which came from Darcy that night. They were not sure of his words, but they all said that the sound was one of pleasure. Only she, Rebecca and Rogers were aware of Mrs. Darcy's condition, and Mrs. Reynolds could imagine the sounds of delight coming from her Master came from his receiving the news which Elizabeth had told her was to be his Christmas present.

Mrs. Reynolds was concerned about Darcy's reaction, for she knew how deeply he had taken the loss of his mother when Georgiana was born. She was afraid that he would be frightened at Elizabeth's news, afraid of her dying from her condition. This is why she had told Elizabeth to delay telling him until the quickening. After the midwife had confirmed Elizabeth's condition, the ladies decided it was time to let Darcy know.

Mr. and Mrs. Darcy did not return to the world the following day, as they stayed in their private world. Neither had a desire to leave it, neither wished to part from the other. Trays of food were taken to them, they lingered in a bath together for a long time, and they took turns loving and sleeping with each other. Only due to their family members arriving in two days and many plans to be handled did they part.

Chapter 19

The morning they emerged from their paradise, they walked to breakfast hand in hand. The glow on Elizabeth's face was remarkable and the smile on Darcy's face was never seen by his staff before. His dimples were in full bloom with pride. Georgiana saw them enter the breakfast room as she ate her eggs. What she witnessed was amazing to her, and she sat staring at them for several moments, as her hand was frozen in mid air with her next bite of breakfast. Darcy noticed his sister and laughed. "Georgiana, have you seen Medusa? You have turned to stone."

"William, I am amazed at you is all. I have never seen you like this. What is going on? Am I to believe this is all from Elizabeth being pleased with her Christmas gift?"

Darcy took Elizabeth's hand in his, lifting it up to his lips as he placed several lingering kisses on it. "William, what is come over you? Have you gone mad behaving so for all to see?"

"I have indeed gone mad, dear sister. Mad with love. Love for the mother of my child. My Christmas gift was even greater than my plans for Elizabeth."

Looking at her sister, Georgiana squealed with delight as she ran to the couple. Embracing them both, Georgiana began to cry. "Such wonderful news. William, you will be the best of fathers, as you already have been for me. I am so excited for both of you. A baby, I am going to be an aunt. This is such wonderful news. Elizabeth, I am so happy for you."

"I am pleased that my Christmas gift was well accepted by both of you. Now, William, when you come back down from floating in the clouds, how would you like your eggs?"

The threesome all broke into laughter. "I am not the only one floating in the clouds my love. You were there with me just moments ago, as you are well aware." Darcy smiled at his wife with such pride. "Now, let us eat so that I may start on my lists of what we need to do in preparation of our child."

By the afternoon that day, Darcy had inspected the nursery, made note of all the changes he felt necessary, had servants search the attic for baby items, which he had brought to his study for his inspection. He looked through items, some of which he remembered from when Georgiana was a baby, some items he had never seen before. Elizabeth joined him in the study, as they made over all the items. Darcy was like a child with a candy store open just for him. As he enjoyed himself with the small sized clothes and infant items, Elizabeth could see the love he had and would share with his children. No child could be more wanted, or loved.

Mrs. Reynolds entered the room with one more box, one she had stored specially for this day. "Master William, Mistress Elizabeth, I wish to give you this gift for your child. It is a box of the Darcy history, to be passed on to your blessed child."

Darcy opened the box to find several small nightdresses for an infant and a beautiful blanket. There were some small booties and a tiny hat. Darcy had a quizzical look on his face. "Where did these items come from, Mrs. Reynolds?"

With a tear falling down her cheek, she smiled at him. "From your mother and grandmother. They made them."

Tears began to flow from Elizabeth's eyes, and Darcy sat stunned, holding the blanket in his hands as his fingers ran softly over it. "How?" Was all Darcy could ask.

"When your mother was so ill after your sister was born, she called me to her side. She knew she would not survive, and she asked me to place these items in a box and save them for her first grandchild. She wished to know that the child would have gifts from his or hers grandmother and great grandmother. The clothes were mainly made by your grandmother, Mistress Anne made the blanket."

Now tears began to flow freely from Darcy's eyes. Elizabeth came to her husband, embracing him tightly. "What a wonderful gift your mother has given us. It will be such a pleasure to have a piece of her and your grandmother to wrap our child in."

Elizabeth then did the unusual for the upper circle of society. She embraced her housekeeper. "Our thanks Mrs. Reynolds for keeping this safe for our child. You are a special part of our family and we are so grateful."

Mrs. Reynolds patted Elizabeth on the back as she embraced the young lady who had made so many changes in the Darcys' lives. "Keeping these safe for your bundle was no duty, it was done out of love." The housekeeper then left the room, drying her eyes on her way.

Chapter 20

Mary had an easy confinement, giving birth to the first grandson of Lord and Lady Matlock. Mrs Bennet insisted on being with her daughter through her labor, though her excitable nature stressed Mary's nerves near breaking. Mr Bennet and Lord Matlock kept the distraught father to be plied with port until Richard was unable to pace any further.

When led to his wife's side, Richard noted the bedding and towels that were being removed from the room. By the time Richard had stepped near the bed, between the spirits from their fathers and the sight of the blood which had come from his wife, Colonel Richard Fitzwilliam, battle hardened leader of soldiers and war hero, found himself fainted to the floor. He awoke on the bed next to his wife, who was holding their son, and there was a cool cloth on his forehead where a knot had developed from his head striking the floor. Groaning, Richard begged everyone to keep his fainting from his brothers, for he knew that Darcy and Bingley would never allow him to live it down, not to mention what his brother Matthew would have to say.

Unfortunately for Richard, Darcy and Elizabeth arrived sooner than expected and, when ushered into the bedchambers, found Richard still nursing his headache. "It is good that you have resigned your commission, as becoming faint over the sight of blood would end up losing battles for England and we would all be speaking French at this very moment." Darcy chided.

When Bingley arrived shortly after, he remarked that if England lost all its battles to France, it might make it easier to obtain good French spirits.

"Just remember, when your wives give birth to your children, it could be you who finds themselves on the floor as well." Richard stated in an irritated voice.

Both Bingley and Darcy refrained from any further teasing. "What name have you decided to bestow on this fine, strapping young man?" Darcy inquired.

Mary looked at her husband. "We have decided to name him Henry Thomas Fitzwilliam. And we would be honored if you and Lizzy would be Henry's godparents."

Darcy was holding his wife's hand and squeezed it as he looked into her eyes. Seeing her nod, Darcy accepted the honor for both of them.

Lady Matlock was thrilled with her grandson, and had purchased so many items for him that it was nearly necessary for them to have another carriage bring the gifts. Her husband complained that he was only allowed in the carriage if he held a stack of gifts. Mary laughed as Lady Matlock showed them all that she had found, blankets, dressing gowns, booties, toys, a small toy horse which appeared to have resembled the first horse Richard had ever had.

Mrs Bennet was equally proud, though she would be even more so when her elder daughters did their duty to their husbands and gave them heirs. Mr Bennet had been secretly spending time in the dowager house at Longbourn where he was making cradles for his grandchildren. The one for Mary's son was carved with a knotwork design around the top. The one he made for Lizzy, which he refused to show to his favorite daughter, was carved with ivy around the top. Thomas Bennet had a strong feeling that Lizzy was carrying a daughter, though he would not speak of such with his wife.

Elizabeth was sleeping in her husband's arms when the first pains began. She grasped Darcy's arm tightly until the pain passed. Darcy woke, confused as to what was happening. Being nearly two in the morning, the household was asleep. For a slumbering household, it woke into full swing in a matter of minutes of the Master calling for Mrs Reynolds and to have the midwife summoned.

While waiting, Mrs Reynolds insisted that Elizabeth walk as much as possible. Her husband insisted on walking by her side, step by step, only stopping when another pain would cause her to not be able to take a step.

"Mrs Reynolds, the babe is not due for two more weeks. This is too soon for the child to be delivered, is it not?"

"Master William, do not fret. Babies will be born when they are ready, not when we tell them. Two weeks is not too long a time to be born early. My own son was born three weeks early, and look what a health, young man he has turned out to be."

"William, there is one bonus to our having the babe now. Mamma is not....ooooh....here to be under foot. Poor Mary had to endure...ooooh....so much of Mamma's fluttering, I am sure I...arggg...would strangle Mamma, if she were here right now."

Darcy laughed. "Even in the agony of giving birth, you find something impertinent to say. Oh, my dear, lovely, Lizzy. I do so love you."

The next pains came closer than the last one had. The labor continued to come quicker and quicker until Mrs Reynolds said it was time to prepare for delivery. The midwife still had not arrived and Mrs

Reynolds was becoming somewhat nervous.

A message arrived stating that Mrs Walker, the midwife, was delivering another baby and unable to come. Mrs Reynolds sent for Mrs Findlay, the cook, to come assist with the delivery.

When they laid Elizabeth on the bed, Mrs Reynolds insisted that Darcy leave the room. He refused, stating he would not leave his wife. Over and over, Mrs Reynolds insisted, telling him that it was improper for him to be in the room when his child was born.

"If you do not allow me to remain with my wife, I will remove all of you and deliver my child by myself." Darcy ranted.

"Now, are you remaining to assist my wife, or should I take charge?"

Knowing Darcy as she had for most of his life, Mrs Reynolds determined it was not worth any further arguments. As Elizabeth's pains grew in intensity, Mrs Reynolds made ready for the delivery.

"Master William, if you are remaining here, then sit behind your wife and allow her to rest against you. When the pain starts, Mrs Darcy, you must bear down and push with all of your might."

Darcy quickly moved behind his wife, wrapping his arms around her to hold her hands. As the pain came, she grasped his hands with a strength Darcy never would have believed she had. Screaming loudly, Elizabeth pushed until she collapsed for a moment. Another pain was quickly upon her and she rallied her strength to push again, drawing strength from her husband. When the pain ended, Mrs Reynolds was crying that the babe was delivered. She quickly handed the infant to the awaiting nursemaid who took the baby to the dressing chamber to be cleansed.

While the babe was being washed and swaddled, Mrs Findlay assisted in massaging Elizabeth's abdomen to encourage the delivery of the afterbirth. Once it had come, the ladies cleaned Elizabeth and then had Darcy move her to the bed in the Master's bedchamber so that the bedding in her room could be changed. The babe was brought to them, placed in Elizabeth's arms.

"You have a daughter, Mrs Darcy." Mrs Reynolds said with a smile. "She is beautiful, just like her mother."

These words caused a great sense of pride in Darcy. "I wished for a daughter with her mother's eyes and smile."

"You are not disappointed?" Elizabeth asked with a raised eyebrow. "Mamma will say that I have failed you by not giving you a son."

"Dearest, there is no entail on Pemberley. I am able to leave my estate to any child I have, son or daughter."

"Are you planning to tease Richard for your having been here for our daughter's birth?"

A wicked grin came to his lips. "Would I do a thing such as that?"

"Yes, William, I know you would do just such a thing. And I believe it will be interesting to watch Richard blush. What should we name our daughter?"

Thinking for a few moments, Darcy finally had a suggestion. "Rose Anne Darcy."

Nodding her head, Elizabeth agreed. "Welcome to the world, Rose. This handsome man is your devoted and loving father."

"And this beautiful woman is your adoring mother." Darcy said as he placed a kiss on his wife's lips.

"Are you truly not disappointed that we have a daughter? It is just Mamma has always said that men needed sons and would be disappointed with daughters."

"Your mother is a fool to think that I would ever be disappointed with any child you give me. I consider myself truly blessed with being the father of your children. Besides." Darcy said with a smile so dazzling that his dimples shone clear. "If your mother insists that we have to have a son, we must do as my Aunt Catherine has always said...Practice."

With a kiss, Darcy wrapped his family in his arms and they fell asleep, their future bright as the morning sun which was shining in the sky.

The End

9629514R00215

Printed in Great Britain
by Amazon.co.uk, Ltd.,
Marston Gate.